LEFT TO FALL

DCI KAREN HEATH CRIME SERIES

JAY NADAL

JOIN MY VIP GROUP

If you haven't already joined, then to say thank you for buying or downloading this book, I'd like to invite you to join my exclusive VIP group where new subscribers get some of my books for FREE. So, if you want to be notified of future releases and special offers ahead of the pack, sign up using the link below:

https://dl.bookfunnel.com/sjhhjs7ty4

Published by 282publishing.com

Copyright @ Jay Nadal 2021

All rights reserved.

Jay Nadal has asserted his right to be identified as the author of this work.

No part of this book may be reproduced, stored in any retrieval system, or transmitted in any form or by any means, electronic, mechanical, photocopying, recording or otherwise, without the prior written permission of the author.

This book is a work of fiction, names, characters, businesses, organizations, places and events other than those clearly in the public domain, are either the product of the author's imagination or used fictitiously. Any resemblance to actual persons, living or dead, events or locales is entirely coincidental.

1

He had walked for hours, traipsing through dense undergrowth, the ground soft, damp and cold. His feet slipped on the lichens and mosses that carpeted the ground beneath his feet. Birch and oak trees stood shoulder to shoulder like guardians of this historic woodland. Night had become day, and with it the imposing and monolithic cliff face loomed into view. It felt like it was crowding in on him from all sides as he craned his neck up to the sky and glimpsed the ragged clifftop with its dense greenery that fringed its edge like an overgrown and bushy eyebrow.

He'd been to this place many times. He had stood at the base of the limestone cliff and watched in awe as fearless climbers scaled its rock face; the crag being a formidable opponent for even the most experienced climbers. The view from the top was just as breathtaking, offering a vista of Gormire Lake, the Vale of York and the Vale of Mowbray that extended as far as the eye could see. A chequered pattern of greenery lit up the landscape on what was another cold and grey morning.

He tugged on the collar of his coat, keen to shield himself from the cold, biting wind that cut through his clothes like icy shards. *This is where it began and where it will end.* Weeks, months and years of humiliation, doubt, and simmering anger led him to this point. His fingers curled into tight fists as he clenched his jaw and stared up at the crag. Eyes narrowing, he scanned the clifftop for any signs of movement. He was alone. He was always alone. The odd sparrowhawk and bullfinch battled through the wind, their outlines nothing more than small dots on the grey canvas above them.

His stomach turned and his breath felt laboured as if his ribs were crushed in a vice. Nature owned his surroundings and possessed the power to take lives. All it took was a footstep in the wrong direction, cramping fingers, or a lack of respect for the loose rocks, and a life could be extinguished in a matter of seconds.

He wasn't going to rely on any of those. The next person to lose their life here would be solely down to him. He should have felt euphoric, but sadness consumed him. *Why was everything so hard?*

The ground rustling behind him tore him from his thoughts. He spun on his heel, his eyes darting from left to right looking for any signs of movement. There were no voices, no walkers, no climbers. He let out a breath he'd been holding for a few minutes, though his heart still hammered in his chest. It was probably a mouse or a rat looking for food. If they hung around long enough, he'd be able to give them a first-class dining experience.

It felt like a few minutes, but glancing at his watch, he realised he'd been rooted to the spot for nearly an hour. He let out a deep sigh and shrugged his shoulders before continuing his journey. Fallen twigs crackled beneath his feet as he made his way towards the cliff, before disappearing out of sight, the woods swallowing him up and camouflaging him from view.

2

"Tights! For crying out loud, do I not own a pair of tights that don't look as if they have been worn after a night of drunken sex and a fall through the bushes," Karen fumed, as she rummaged through one of the drawers, scattering socks and tights on the floor all around her. Every pair she pulled out either had a ladder, was stretched, or had a ripped and saggy gusset.

Frustration simmered beneath the surface as Karen darted around her room searching for something to wear. Her recent move to York left her surrounded by half empty removal boxes, bubble wrap and packing tissue. The rental apartment was more than adequate for her needs, but as she glanced around it looked as if the removal men had literally dumped her possessions everywhere. Bubble wrap hung over the edge of opened boxes, the smell of cardboard lingered in the air, and scrunched up balls of packing tissue surrounded an overspilling black bin liner in one corner of the room.

Everything was such a whirlwind in her mind. The transition to York had been bumpy to say the least. Following the death of her sister, Karen had taken a few weeks off as compassionate leave. She'd spent time with her parents, packed away Jane's belongings from her room, shared a tearful goodbye with Nurse Robyn Allen, and done a lot of soul-searching. London had been good to her, but in equal measure carried many painful memories. The opportunity to start afresh in a new part of the country was both appealing and daunting.

Karen also used the opportunity to spend a few days in York with Zac. He'd been the perfect host as he'd showed her all the tourist hotspots. Karen had seen inside York Minster, the stunning cathedral she'd only marvelled at from a distance. Together they'd walked along the city's mediaeval walls for what felt like miles, snaked through the Shambles, a narrow 14th century thoroughfare with lovely overhanging timber-framed buildings, and dined at Delrio's, Zac's favourite Italian restaurant.

They had shared a few evenings together which had given Karen the chance to know Zac and Summer away from work. Though they'd had a laugh and eaten way too much, Karen and Zac had used the time to talk about their feelings. To begin with Zac and Karen had been hesitant, keeping their cards closely pressed to their chests, which had made conversations a bit clunky.

Karen had rolled her eyes when Zac had not so romantically blurted out "we're not getting any younger!" He'd spoken about them giving it a go, to which Karen had agreed. For once Karen was stepping out of her comfort zone with a "fuck it" attitude.

She now found herself in York knee-deep in boxes, and a ball of anxiety that still sat within her. The transition into the North Yorkshire Police had been easier than anticipated. Detective Superintendent Laura Kelly, "the Terminator", had been more than helpful, smoothing her entry into the force as promised with Karen being reinstated to DCI.

Everything was falling into place apart from the simple task of finding a bloody pair of tights. Karen rummaged through another box of underwear. "Too thick! Nope, too thin," she moaned, tossing aside various unopened packets. Her eyes widened when she picked up a pack of green tights. "*Green!* Really? Where the fuck would I wear green tights?" Maybe she'd needed them for a fancy-dress party or something once, but her sensibility had overruled her impulsive and frankly ridiculous purchase. Karen tossed the pack towards the bin.

She wanted to make a good impression in her first few weeks on the job. Karen dressed smartly, more befitting for her title, especially as Laura had taken time out to introduce Karen to the top team in the North Yorkshire police force. At times she was left embarrassed as senior officers welcomed her with open arms, gloating over the fact they had bagged a senior officer from the Met who came with a vast array of operational experience and managing large teams.

One thing that Karen hadn't bargained for was how cold it was in Yorkshire. Biting winds and sub-zero temperatures left her chilled to the bone.

Resigned to the fact that most of her underwear and tights now littered the floor, Karen gave up on the skirt and jacket combo, and swapped it out for trousers and a tight-fitting jumper.

"Manky... Where are you?" Karen shouted as she raced

through the rooms. "Now is not the time to be playing bloody games you monster." Karen kissed her lips a few times to get his attention. She finally heard him meow from behind the boxes stacked in the corner of the lounge. She smiled peering around them. "You've made yourself a cosy little den there haven't you?" She bent down and stroked him. "I've got to dash now; I'll see you later."

Karen poked her head into the kitchen to double-check there was enough food and water for Manky before she threw on her coat and grabbed the car keys, slamming the door behind her.

3

"I thought *I* panicked over clutter!" Karen teased as she walked around Jade's apartment and stared wide-eyed at the pristine and expansive size of the place. "You've taken your OCD to a new level. It's spotless. You should see my place. It's a pig's shithole in comparison."

Since Karen had already made the decision to move to York for the foreseeable future, her new boss, Laura, had followed through on her promises and let Karen form her own team. She'd cherry-picked a few officers from the Dennis Bailey case where she and Zac had finally tracked down and captured a serial killer behind a string of savage and brutal murders.

Not long after deciding to leave, Karen had sat with Jade to tell her about the move. Shock was soon followed by sadness as the reality of their partnership ending hit Jade. However, Karen had offered her a silver lining. The offer of a move to York to continue their partnership, and the mentoring to equip her to be a DI.

Jade hadn't been expecting the offer, but with no family ties or partner holding her in London, it hadn't taken much convincing for Jade to jump at the chance. She'd travelled with Karen to meet Detective Superintendent Laura Kelly, which provided an opportunity for Jade to get a feel of the city, the working environment, and Laura.

It had been a no-brainer in Jade's eyes. Having taken a tour, she understood why Karen gushed in her phone calls about the offices, facilities, and working environment. Jade had been equally impressed by those she'd met, and how laid-back and professional they were. It was in marked contrast to the frenetic lifestyle of living and working in London.

Jade had opted for a two-bedroom apartment in Holgate, north-west of the city centre. Karen's apartment in comparison was smaller, offered her only one bedroom and cost her considerably more than Jade's.

"I've been seen off with my apartment," Karen started as she wandered from room to room, peeking in through doorways, opening cupboard doors and generally being a nosey parker.

"No, Karen, they saw you coming. They can charge what they like in the city centre. It's premium real estate. I'm two miles away from you, exactly eight minutes' drive, and I pay five hundred pounds less than you and I get an extra bedroom." Jade tipped her head to one side and shrugged her shoulders, looking pleased with herself.

"Mine looks bigger because I've unpacked everything. I hate mess," Jade continued.

"Don't tell me it's the girl guide in you! Organised, methodical, practical."

Jade didn't rise to the jibe as she sorted out her bag for the day. Though Karen had been in York for three weeks now, Jade had only been there for a week and was still finding her feet. She'd spent most of her time unpacking and getting her apartment in shape.

"I've been so rushed off my feet that I haven't chilled. A friend at uni came from York and she always raved about the place. I've got a long list of recommendations."

Karen raised a brow. "That's fantastic. Maybe you can hook up with her this weekend and she can show you around. I did that with Zac a while back, and there was so much to see."

Jade shook her head. "Vicky, my friend, didn't return to York. She studied environmental sciences and biology. The lucky sod bagged a job in Devon. A company that deals with the investigation and protection of marine life," Jade said, clicking her fingers in the air as she tried to remember the name of the company.

"I'm sure she'll be back up here every so often, if her family is still here?" Karen asked as she leant over and flicked through a stack of magazines on the coffee table.

Jade nodded. "For sure."

"In the meantime, how about if we do the touristy thing on Saturday, work permitting?" Karen offered, now eyeing up the prints on a wall beside her. "There's still tons that I want to see. And I know of a fantastic Italian that Zac took me to. And *you* know how much we love Italian. We could do a tourist trail and then grab dinner?"

"Yeah, that would be great. Belinda seems nice. I've been

invited back to hers one evening this week for a beer, pizza and Netflix night. So that should be fun."

Karen smiled. A part of her had been worried that Jade would feel alone, especially if Karen was spending some of her spare time with Zac.

Karen glanced at the time on her phone. "Come on, Jade, I know how much you love talking, but we really do need to get to work."

Jade's eyes widened in mock disgust. "I've been ready for ages. It's you that hasn't stopped gassing. Let's go! Anyone would think you're presenting *Through The Keyhole*. Does the place meet with your approval?" Jade asked, waving an accusatory finger in Karen's direction as she grabbed her coat and made for the door.

4

As her hands gripped the steering wheel, Karen still couldn't get her head around the fact that she was driving to work every day. Her commute was no more than ten to fifteen minutes, and she could reach most parts of the city in less than thirty, a far cry from the long slog she had faced every day travelling into London on the Central line.

Today was Jade's first day, but Karen was determined to make sure that Jade felt both excited and supported to be starting a new job. "Any nerves about today?" she asked.

Jade stared out of her passenger window as her eyes darted from one city sight to another. Since she knew London like the back of her hand, settling into a new city made her feel like the new kid starting school. Not only would she have to learn the quirks of the city but also start building a criminal profile on who the bad apples were, the toughest and roughest parts of the city, the level of crime, who the major crime families were, who was instrumental in leading the county line drug operations, as well as high-profile ex-offenders.

She watched a little girl hop along the road beside her mum. Her brown ponytail bobbed up and down as she played an imaginary game of dodge the lines between paving slabs. Her little hand grasped a small blue school bag as she smiled and belted out a playground song. *Such beautiful innocence*, Jade thought as her lips curled into a smile.

"A little," she finally answered having been dragged from her thoughts. "I always felt sorry for the new kid who joined the school year midway through. Friendship circles had already been established, and they would often find it hard making friends. It kinda feels like that."

Karen sensed the uncertainty and vulnerability in Jade's voice. She'd felt a little of that when joining Zac's team to track down Dennis Bailey.

"You'll be fine. They are a really good bunch. Besides, you've met one or two of them already. And I'm sure they'll make you feel at home in much the same way they did when I first came up here."

Jade nodded firmly, maintaining an air of confidence, even though she felt the first tentacles of anxiety tickle her stomach. She had been pleasantly surprised by Belinda's friendliness when Karen had been showing her around. The fact the woman had gone out of her way to extend her hospitality to a complete stranger wasn't lost on Jade as her smile returned.

"What have you got on at the moment?" Jade asked as Karen pulled up at the lights.

"It's been pretty quiet recently, to be honest. We've got a suspicious death that we're looking into. A homeless man found dead. Badly beaten. You'll be getting stuck into that."

"Is that it?"

"At the moment. It's not like London where we have murders every day. There's still your fair share of antisocial behaviour, violent and organised crime, county lines, murders and everything else in between but just not the volume we've been used to."

"So more time to investigate each crime."

"Exactly, Jade. It means their clear-up rate is much better, and that's music to my ears. But South Yorkshire wants us to get involved in a human trafficking ring. They've had three Chinese illegals murdered. Two men and a woman. Bound, gagged, and hacked to death. They believe the ringleaders could be camped out in our area. We're waiting on intel to confirm that."

"Were the victims destined for Yorkshire?" Jade questioned.

Karen shook her head and pulled off as the lights turned green. "I'm not entirely sure. From what I can gather, the SIO leading the case believes that they were being trafficked to Manchester. In the past they've been taken straight into the suburbs, but officers have been proactive in covert operations to break the ring. So, they're diverting the alleged victims through Yorkshire first. There was even talk that a premiership footballer had been caught with one of the victims in a knocking shop."

Jade groaned in disgust and swore.

"Exactly. Thankfully, they dismantled some of the ring. But it wasn't Chinese nationals being trafficked, it was Czech nationals tied up in the ring and forced into the sex trade. Women were being pimped out twelve hours a day for as little as ten quid a time on the streets of Levenshulme and Longsight, and if they didn't earn enough, the ringleaders would starve them." Karen tapped her steering wheel in time with a song on the radio.

"The men didn't fare much better," Karen added, as she drove through the gates of the police compound and made her way to the small cluster of car parks that dotted the complex and parked up. "Most of them were beaten to a pulp and forced to work long hours in South Manchester car washes. They finally busted a few houses in Gorton and rescued the victims."

5

The wave of warm air bathed their faces the second Karen and Jade walked through the doors of their building to the newly formed specialist crime unit, or SCU. Karen glanced across to Jade and widened her eyes as if to say "here we go". Jade smiled before drawing in a deep breath to steady the anticipatory nerves that twisted her insides.

Karen smiled as another officer passed them carrying a wad of files in one hand and a mug of steaming liquid in the other. The smell of freshly brewed coffee tickled her nose and stirred her taste buds. She was desperate for a caffeine fix, but it would have to wait.

Karen guided Jade towards a small office where a civilian officer sat busily tapping away on her keyboard. A camera and screen were positioned towards the far end of the room, and whilst Jade went inside to get her new ID card set up, Karen took the opportunity to pop along to see Laura.

Detective Superintendent Laura Kelly had her head down

and was running her pen along a document when Karen appeared in the doorway. She waited for a moment before tapping on the open door. Laura bucked her head up in surprise and leant back. "Karen, sorry, I didn't know you were hovering. Neck deep in a speech I'm preparing for a conference next week."

"That's okay, ma'am. I wanted to check in and let you know that Jade has arrived, and I'll settle her in this morning."

"Fantastic. Thanks for letting me know. It's great to bolster the team further with another experienced officer."

Laura paused for a moment to study Karen, which led to an awkward silence hanging in the air. Karen folded her arms and grimaced, not knowing what to say, nor wanting her arms to dangle by her sides like strings of loose spaghetti.

"I know you've been here a few weeks now. How are *you* settling in? Are you happy with your team?"

Karen eyed Laura with suspicion. She'd only been asked the same question a week ago, and her response would be no different.

"I'm fine, ma'am. Lots to learn. I'm still working out the individual strengths of each of the officers on my team, so I know how best to use them. They're a fantastic bunch, and I'm very lucky to have them. Having Jade on board will help a lot with that."

Laura nodded, before resting her elbows on the desk and forming a steeple with her fingers. "I know you've been through a difficult period, what with the loss of your sister. I want to make sure that you have the right support in place and enough time to come to terms with it, so it doesn't impact your work. We want you getting off to a good start, don't we?"

Karen felt her body stiffen. They'd gone over this last week, so she wasn't sure why Laura was raising it again.

"Ma'am, I can assure you that I'm absolutely fine. I've done my grieving. I'm excited about what the future holds, and fully focused on the job in hand. New start and all of that. I'm keen to get the team stuck into a meaty case to see how they perform. I'll be watching all of them closely to see who works well together, what their individual strengths are and how best to utilise them."

Laura returned a smile, but Karen could tell that there was no warmth or sincerity behind it. It was functional.

"Excellent. Well, as you know, my door is always open. I like to take a keen interest in all of my team. The buck stops with me, so I don't want anything, and I mean *anything* both inside and outside of the office affecting the reputation of my unit. If there's anything that you need then you only have to ask. And I mean anything… Now I'd love to chat, but really need to get back to the speech."

"Yes, ma'am." Karen turned, holding a polite smile until she returned to the corridor.

Is this "the Terminator" flashing a hint of the abrasiveness and directness I've heard so much about? She hadn't figured out Laura yet. There were times Laura had been warm, friendly, and approachable. And at other times, she could have given a block of ice a run for its money. Karen had already formed the opinion that she would have to tread carefully around Laura until she had sized her up properly.

6

Karen did her hardest to brush off the discussion with Laura, but the clipped tone gnawed away at her. She pushed it to the back of her mind before grabbing Jade and making her way to the SCU.

"I can't get over how beautiful these offices are," Jade gushed, peering through the glass panelling that lined the corridor.

"I know. It makes a change from what we've been used to back in London, hey?"

Jade didn't reply but nodded enthusiastically. She looked down at her appearance to make sure everything was in place. She wore a grey two-piece skirt and jacket combo with a white blouse beneath. A necklace with glassy black beads hung low around her neck. Seconds before they walked through the door, Jade ran her fingers through her short dark hair, and pushed the sides around her ears which made her look even more impish.

"Ready?" Karen asked, rubbing Jade's back.

"As ready as I'll ever be."

Karen pushed open the door to the SCU. The silence and softness of the corridor was replaced with a low murmur of conversations, and the rhythmic tapping of keyboards from officers and civilian staff. Somewhere in the distance, the repetitive swooshing of paper rolling off a photocopier added to the ambient noise.

Karen stopped by a spare desk which butted up against DC Belinda Webb's. Belinda looked up and then rose from her chair to come around and shake Jade's hand.

"Great to see you again, skip," Belinda offered, her smile warm and heartfelt, as was the shake of her hand.

"Thanks. I'm looking forward to working with you… and having that pizza and beer night." Jade laughed to break the ice, with Belinda joining her.

"Before we get too comfortable, I want to introduce you to two other officers," Karen interrupted glancing around the office.

DCs Tyler Owen and Ed Hyde were stood by Tyler's desk when Karen walked over, with Jade and Belinda in tow.

"Tyler… Ed… You two weren't here when Jade came into the office last time. This is DS Jade Whiting, and your new DS."

Tyler and Ed both stepped forward, jostling like kids for position, each keen to be the first to get into Jade's good books. Ed had the advantage and got to her first. He was impeccably dressed and well-spoken as always. He introduced himself with a strong, exuberant, and firm handshake that went on far longer than necessary. It left Jade holding in a burst of laughter that threatened to escape. She glanced across to Karen, who rolled her eyes as if to suggest "he means no harm... you'll get used to him".

The first thing that Jade noticed about Tyler was his big, pearly white grin against his dark skin and the fact that he towered over her by at least a foot.

"Good to meet you, skip. We've heard a lot about you, and I can't speak about the others, but I'm certainly looking forward to working with you." He laughed as he threw a cheeky glance at the others.

"Me too," Jade replied, looking at those assembled around her. "I've heard a lot of good things about all of you. I'd like to sit down with each of you individually at some point in the next day or two to find out more about you and get a feel for how you guys work both individually and as a team."

Tyler nodded enthusiastically; his charismatic white smile still firmly plastered on his face.

"Belinda, can you get Jade settled in for me, and I'll catch up with all of you in a bit?"

Belinda nodded before heading back to her desk.

As Karen left, she leant into Tyler who watched Jade walk off. "Tyler, roll your tongue back in! Don't even think about it. Jade's your skip," Karen teased, before playfully punching him in the arm.

7

Karen darted out of the front door of the building and hurried along the pathway towards the next block. She wrapped her arms around her chest and grimaced as the cold wind swirled. She was still getting used to what officers termed "the camp". Karen could see why as it reminded her of a military barracks. It consisted of a cluster of two- and three-storey buildings interconnected by walkways slap bang in the middle of dense greenery, with mature trees and grassed areas that skirted all the pathways.

Though the trees were bare, their bony finger-like branches reached towards the grey skies. Karen looked forward to the first signs of spring a few weeks away and the warmth the new season would bring.

The adjoining building was practically the same in configuration. As she pushed through the glass doors, they glided gently across the carpeted floors with the slightest hint of a *swoosh* as they closed.

Zac sat behind his desk when Karen poked her head around the door.

"Boo!" she shouted.

Zac shook his head and laughed. "I don't know if it slipped your mind, but my room has three glass walls and I saw you six feet away before you turned into the doorway…"

Karen rolled her eyes. "Doh! You could still play the game, spoilsport." She dropped herself into the chair opposite him. "There's no harm in a bit of silliness every so often?"

Zac mirrored her smile as they stared at each other for a few minutes.

"Stop it. Stop looking at me like that."

Zac smirked. "I can't help it if I fancy you, and I look forward to seeing you in the mornings."

Karen let out a sigh. Everything had happened so quickly she hadn't caught her breath yet. In the space of a few months her life had been flipped on its head. The sadness and grief which had gripped her had eased in recent weeks spent with Zac as their working relationship had blossomed into a fledgling *something* that neither of them had expected. Whatever it was, they didn't care, but they certainly enjoyed how it made them feel.

"How's Jade?" he asked.

"She's put on a brave face, but I know she's nervous as fuck. I'm sure she'll be fine. The team seem to have taken to Jade, especially Tyler, and Bel is settling her in."

Zac laughed. "Good ol' Tyler. He fancies his chances with most women he meets. A flash of pearly white teeth, a charming smile, and a few chat-up lines and he thinks he's

Adonis. He's harmless really, but you've got to love a trier."

Karen puckered her lips in disappointment. "He didn't flirt with me…"

"That's because you're old enough to be his mum."

"You cheeky git. I'm not that old."

Zac shrugged. "Debatable to be honest."

"You're treading on thin ice, *Mr Walker*…"

"Anyway, I'm sure having you around will help with the transition, and then she'll be firing on all cylinders."

Karen nodded and agreed. "Right. Now that you've made me feel really old and past it, I've got to dash back, but I wanted to pick your brain on the homeless death that we are dealing with at the moment. I remember you saying last week that you'd have a think about it as you had a few ideas."

Zac locked his hands behind his head and flapped his arms whilst staring at the ceiling to gather his thoughts. He rolled his tongue across his teeth before his eyes widened. "Ah, yes. I remember dealing with a case a while back where a homeless man had been beaten to within an inch of his life. It was a drug-related thing."

"Right…?" Karen interrupted. "And?"

Zac was still pulling thoughts from the deepest part of his memory. "There was a crack house that we shut down where a lot of the homeless used to go to score. One of the main dealers was a dickhead called Alfie Barton. He's got previous for assault and dealing. You'll find him on the system. He doesn't like us as you can imagine."

"Was he connected?"

Zac nodded. "He'd supply a bit of gear to the homeless for free and hook them in. In return, he'd get the poor sods to deal for him. If they were caught with his gear, he'd get off and let them carry the can. I remember our victim was homeless and one of Alfie's dealers. Sadly for him he'd decided to pocket some of the cash…"

"And Alfie made an example of your victim?" Karen said.

"Yep. You might want to see if your victim had any connections with Alfie. I think Tyler had run-ins with Alfie a few months ago, so have a word with him."

Karen rose from her chair and headed for the door. "Great, I'm about to have a quick update with the team, so I wanted to touch base with you first. I'll catch up with you later. Thanks for your help."

8

Karen gathered the team around the incident board. Tyler, Ed, Belinda and now Jade formed an apron around her, with various support and civilian staff forming a second tier as they perched on any available desk space.

"Right, before we kick off, I hope you had a good weekend and are ready to start the week fit and well. I also wanted to take the opportunity to introduce the newest member of our team." Karen stepped forward and stood by Jade. "This is DS Jade Whiting for any of you that haven't met her yet. Jade is joining us from the Met Police and was my DS in the MIT. When you get a moment, track Jade down and introduce yourselves to her. I promise she won't bite."

Jade cheek's flushed red as laughter rippled amongst the team.

"We've got a lot to get on with today, and our focus still needs to be on identifying anyone connected with Aleem Noor. Jade, the team can bring you up to speed with the victim. But in a nutshell Aleem was twenty-eight years old, a Syrian refugee in the UK for three years."

"Homeless for all that time?" Jade asked, her mind already dialled into the investigation.

Karen nodded. "How he got to York is still a bit of a grey area for us. The little we do know is that he was in York for at least the last twelve to eighteen months. We're not sure where he was before that." Karen turned towards Belinda. "Bel, what's the latest?"

Belinda backtracked in her notepad for a few pages. "We are still short on witnesses. No one saw or heard anything. We've conducted door-to-door enquiries with shops in the area close to where Aleem's body was found. CCTV footage has been secured from shopkeepers."

"Have we started to go through it?"

Belinda shook her head.

"Okay, we'll do that next. Ed?"

"Karen, we've not been able to find any next of kin. Certainly not in this country anyway. We've put in a request to speak to someone at the Syrian Embassy, as well as the British Red Cross. As yet, we haven't been able to identify whether he came across officially, or in the back of a lorry."

Karen puffed out her cheeks. The case had been going on for a week now, and with little progress to report, it hadn't been a good start for her when she was so keen to impress. A news appeal last week had generated a few leads, but her officers still faced a wall of silence from the homeless community. She had witnessed it countless times, a deep-seated hate and fear of the police amongst the homeless.

Though the police were there to help them, the homeless community was just that, a community which kept to themselves, and lived by the rules of the street.

"Any further DNA or forensic evidence from the victim?" Karen asked as she turned towards pictures of Aleem Noor. His face resembled an out of shape football — kicked and stamped upon with such ferocity his skull had shattered in nine places. Further injuries included two fractured eye sockets, a broken jaw, and three broken teeth.

Belinda continued. "Forensics were able to identify partial footprint impressions from the side of Noor's face. Other than that, nothing else. Oh, he had a lice infestation in his hair both on his head and in his pubic region."

"Blimey, that's fucking gross," an officer muttered. "That's put me off my breakfast," he added, wrapping up the remains of his bacon roll and tossing it into the nearest bin, his face a shade or two paler than it had been a few minutes ago.

Karen was thinking the same and felt like gagging.

Ed chipped in. "We know the cause of death was severe bleeding on the brain, and there were no signs of a weapon being used as part of the assault, nor were any found by the search teams. So, our only hope is that something was captured on CCTV footage."

Karen nodded. "Let's start with that first."

9

Beth had been eyeing up this crag for a while now in her unofficial bucket list of climbs. Now on her way back up the rocky face, she took a moment to think back on the exhilaration she'd experienced on the way down. Far better than she'd ever imagined it would be. Ideally, she would have preferred to have delayed scaling this difficult cliff for a couple of months, but she was desperate to enter a competition for amateur climbers in Oregon, USA in six weeks' time.

Morning dew still clung to the shrubs, wild grasses, and trees that had lined her route to the crag. As she carefully picked her way back up, the rock face was more slippery than she would have liked, but that added to the thrill and excitement of pushing her body and mind beyond her comfort zone.

Breathtaking was the word that had sprung to her mind as she swivelled on her rope and admired the landscape behind her. Gormire Lake, fringed by an apron of dense woodland, stared back at her like a darkened Cyclops eye.

Beyond it a patchwork quilt of shades of green and brown fields extended towards the horizon, where it merged into the grey low-level clouds that hugged the hilltops.

Whitestone Cliff presented a true test for her, but once she reached the summit, the tough ascent would be worth the difficulty. This was the largest crag in the North Yorkshire Moors and a challenge for most intermediate and experienced climbers. Characterised by mainly steep committing lines on predominantly friable rock, it came with areas of fragile stability. She'd spent the day before deciding on her best route. The unlikely looking Gauche and the stupendous Night Watch were suggested as good introductions to the crag on reasonably stable rock.

During her pre-climb research, she'd identified the right location by a bench which had been mentioned in countless climbing blogs. To the right of the bench would be her spot where a gully steepened towards its base. Beth had listened to fellow climbers on Facebook groups who'd pointed out that it was customary to take a spare rope and set up an abseil from a convenient tree to protect the descent.

Muscles contracting and blood pumping, Beth realised how much she loved the challenge of the ascent. The towers and walls jutted out. The slabs leant back, inviting her to climb them. Though she had been climbing for many years the first signs of cramp stiffened her fingers. Beth leant to the right and draped her chest and forearms across the sloping shelf before catching her right toe on a polished hold. She pressed up with one arm and reached for the next small ledge.

Beth glanced down for a second and noticed how the ground sloped steeply from beneath the overhang, emphasising the exposure. She finally let go with the other hand

and swung into the unknown. Her hand jam slipped out, but she swiftly stabbed her other hand safely back into a horizontal crack, grateful for its rough texture.

"You can do this. You've got this, Beth," she whispered gasping for breath.

Though her body trembled slightly, her determination pushed on as she inched up the rope, which now dropped away from her and out of sight. Though the angle was now easier, her strength was beginning to wane, so the journey was slow and steady. With just metres to go, she stopped and enjoyed the moment. Breathing freely, she glanced towards the top before craning her head to look at the view behind her. She smiled and took in everything that North Yorkshire had to offer.

Having caught her breath, she pushed on, but paused as soon as the line shifted and slackened slightly. Beth glanced up towards the cliff edge, wondering if the rock had shifted, or if the line had slipped over a jutting edge. There was always a risk of loose rock shaking free and falling. Her first thoughts were to scan her surroundings in case debris was coming her way. She tugged on her rope to make sure it was still secure, and then continued her climb until she heard a voice.

"I've been waiting for you."

10

Beth froze. The man stood on the ledge, peering down at her. Even through his smile, a coldness settled in his eyes that sent a shiver down Beth's spine. She smiled nevertheless, sensing her precarious position.

"I won't be long. Give me a second and I'll be there." Beth didn't know what to say, so attempted to make idle chit-chat whilst she inched up the remaining few feet.

"I've been waiting for you," he repeated.

By now he had knelt down close to her rope and placed both hands on the ground.

"This is what happens when you let me down. Who's going to freeze now?" he hissed pulling a knife from inside his jacket.

Beth's eyes widened in fear, a million scenarios flooding through her mind. Instinctively she glanced down even though every neuron in her brain screamed not to. Her mouth felt tinder dry as her heart raced.

His thin lips tugged upward at the corners. "All I need to do is cut this rope and you'll be gone. Gone from my memories, my thoughts, and this world."

"Please. I don't know what you want. If you want money, my bag is up there, you can take anything you want. My car keys are there. You can take my car. Please. Just let me get to the top and we can talk about this."

Her body stiffened through fear and cramp. Her fingers clutched and clawed at the rock whilst her toes grappled with the slimy rock face. As her eyes scanned the rock, her mind calculated the quickest way for her to scale the remaining distance with the necessary momentum.

He sensed the desperation in Beth's voice, which excited him further. "Right now your mind is thinking about your desperate situation, and your survival instincts are kicking in. Fight or flight is gripping your whole body as adrenaline courses through your veins. You're wondering whether you can cover the last few feet before I have time to cut the rope."

Panic smothered Beth as her throat tightened, her eyes reddening through tears and fear. Her hands and feet flailed across the wet surface as she scrambled for the top.

He laughed at the woman's fragility. Only a thin rope kept her from meeting the cold hard surface at the base of the cliff.

"Please, I beg you, please don't do this." Beth's wide gaze locked on the top — only inches away. She could feel the earth on the tips of her fingers even whilst desperation fought to capture her senses.

The man grabbed the rope with one hand and ran his knife through the fragile fibres with the other. The tension in the rope slackened as it fell away. Beth's fingers clung to the earth as the weight of her body pulled her back. *Oh, God! Oh my God!* A guttural scream tore from her throat as she plummeted backward and into the shallow air of the abyss.

The man peered over the edge and studied her shocked face as she raced towards the ground. With wide, terrified eyes, her arms and legs flailed in the air until her body landed with a sickening crack and thump on the ground below.

11

Karen and Jade picked up a coffee from the canteen before making their way to the video evidence room. Parked in front of a large TV screen, they spent the next two hours reviewing footage secured by the team members covering the area of Aleem's attack.

Three of the video feeds had been ruled out after Karen had found no evidence of Aleem. They'd moved on to a full set of recordings taken from a fried chicken takeaway that had cameras positioned inside and outside the shop.

Jade sipped on a coffee whilst Karen fiddled with the scroll wheel, pausing the tape every time a lone figure came into view. She'd already ruled out most of the individuals, though one or two piqued her interest. Having reached the end of one tape she sighed and dropped back in her chair.

"It's a dirty job but someone's got to do it," Karen said, loading the next flash drive into the computer.

She hoped this one would be promising as it belonged to

the city's security cameras. Operators had informed Karen's team they had identified footage containing Aleem and chopped together recordings from various cameras to track his path.

Karen pressed play and within seconds a short clip picked up a man walking slowly along one of the quieter side streets in town. Karen narrowed her eyes. She noticed how the man stayed close to each of the shopfronts, and at times bumped into them before staggering away.

Jade held up pictures of Aleem. "The images are too dark and grainy to even know if it's a match."

Karen agreed but pushed on regardless. It only took a few minutes before another camera captured Aleem's face as he passed beneath a street light. "That's a clear shot," Karen pointed out. She looked again at the photo. Karen nodded. "Yep, I'd say that shows a strong resemblance, don't you?"

"I agree."

The camera tracked his drunken stagger through the town before dropping out of sight. At times his progress was so slow that it looked as if he'd stopped to stand still. At one point during the recordings, Aleem veered to his right and stumbled into discarded rubbish left out by one of the shopkeepers. Aleem tripped over it before landing on the pile and rolling off before slowly getting to his feet. The odd pedestrian gave him a wide berth, viewing him with suspicion before they crossed the road to distance themselves.

He's in a pretty bad way. I wonder if he even knows where he's heading? Jade thought.

When three male figures walked in the same direction but on the other side of the street, Karen sat up in her chair.

Frustratingly, Aleem also took a left down a side road then turned and disappeared out of sight at that exact moment. The men appeared to be larking around, jostling each other and kicking at the discarded boxes left out by shopkeepers in readiness for the refuse collection the next morning. She raised a brow in disapproval and shook her head.

To begin with Karen could pass off the exuberance as anti-social behaviour, but when one of the men pointed over to where Aleem had been a second ago, Karen felt a glimmer of hope. At first one of the men appeared reluctant, pointing as if to suggest they should carry on in the direction they were heading, whilst the other two crossed and went down the same turning.

Karen grabbed a map of the town from her folder and ran a finger along the roads in the video. The side turning Aleem had used was a cut through between two streets. From first impressions, there were no shopfronts or entrances, just the rear of all the properties. Karen assumed there would be little vehicle or foot traffic at most times of the day and night.

"Bollocks." Karen tossed the map to one side and stared at the empty screen. The men quickened their pace to almost a slow jog as they turned and disappeared from sight.

"Is that all we're going to...?" Karen's phone ringing interrupted Jade.

Karen held up a finger as she answered, listening quietly to the caller before raising a brow in Jade's direction. Karen grabbed her pen and scribbled notes down on a pad before confirming they'd attend.

"Jade, get your things together; we've got another suspicious death."

12

Unfamiliar with the area, Karen relied on Belinda to take her and Jade to the location of the incident. Karen still marvelled at how in under an hour she could leave the hustle and bustle of the city and end up in an untamed natural environment where even the air smelt different. Shops and offices were replaced by rolling green landscapes, tall hedgerows, narrow lanes and ploughed fields that extended as far as the eye could see.

Belinda pulled into the visitor centre and stopped wherever she found a spot. Emergency vehicles swarmed the car park as Karen stepped from the car and inhaled a deep breath to savour the soothing earthiness in the air. It felt unspoilt, clean and pure. Several police cars, ambulances, and rescue jeeps had crammed into any available space blocking any civilian vehicles who had unfortunately turned up first.

The chopping of rotor blades hummed above her as Karen glanced up towards the murky skies. After being called, an NPAS helicopter circled overhead. The scale of the resources summoned for this job overwhelmed Karen as small clusters of personnel stood around.

A uniformed officer made his way towards Karen and briefly tipped his head. "Ma'am. Constable Adams."

"What have we got?" Karen asked, buttoning up her coat and stuffing her hands in her pockets.

"We were called about thirty minutes ago when walkers discovered our female victim lying on a small overhanging ledge above ground."

"Did she have any vitals when they found her?"

Adams shook his head as the corners of his mouth turned down. "Negative. She was long gone. The extent of her injuries saw to that. We have officers down there taping off the scene."

Whilst Belinda took witness statements, the officer led Karen and Jade along a path just wide enough for two or three people abreast. The start of the walk was relatively flat and because the car park was quite high up, it made it easy for the officers to wind their way through the shrubs and undergrowth towards the crag.

Jade grimaced as her feet squelched in the muddied earth. She hadn't expected to go on a mini hike where the best footwear would have been a pair of hiking boots.

Karen glanced over at her and smirked. "Welcome to Yorkshire."

"Sorry about the walk, ma'am," Adams said, raising his voice to be heard as the police helicopter dipped its nose and moved away from the scene, its services needed elsewhere. "Unfortunately, we can't get vehicles up here, certainly not ours anyway. Perhaps a 4x4 jeep, yeah."

Karen shrugged as she continued to trudge through the sodden ground, her sixty-pound court shoes useless in these conditions and now totally ruined. "What a waste of a fucking good pair of shoes," she fumed.

"You not got a pair of these?" Adams asked, sticking one of his feet in the air to show off his police issue black Magnum zip boots.

"Not wishing to state the bloody obvious, Adams, but if I had a pair in the boot, do you not think I'd be wearing them now?" Karen replied, rolling her eyes.

The officer cleared his throat and stared ahead before picking up his speed to put a bit of distance between him and Karen.

"Oh my God, look at that view," Jade whispered dreamily. "That's pure English countryside at its best."

Karen had to agree. From the top of the crag the views from Whitestone Cliff were spectacular. Even though it was still a little misty and grey, the view carried for miles. On any other occasion she could have happily sat there for hours letting her mind wander and imagining what it felt like to be a bird floating above this rich green landscape.

They paused by the cliff's edge which was now cordoned off with police tape. From her position Karen couldn't see over the cliff but moved a few feet further along until she could crouch down and peer over. The sheer drop sent her head spinning. She quickly pulled back and took a few deep breaths as cold fear raced through her veins and paralysed her body.

She inched back on her hands and knees until she felt safe enough to stand and move away, much to Adams's amusement who hid his smile behind a hand.

Karen returned to join Jade, who'd taken the sensible decision to stay well away from the cliff edge. She cleared her throat and smiled awkwardly at Jade and Adams knowing what a idiot she must have looked.

Not for the faint-hearted. And certainly not for those with a fear of heights.

13

"The victim appears to have been ascending the crag from this point." Adams pointed to a short length of rope connected to a tree about fifteen feet away from the cliff edge.

"And the rope broke…?" Karen asked, pointing towards the other end that stopped inches short from the edge of the cliff.

Adams shrugged. "We're not entirely sure. It's not safe for us to venture that close."

"We can't examine it?"

Adams shook his head. "Afraid not, ma'am. It's too dangerous to see what's presented on the edge of the rocks. The earth could slip beneath your feet and take you over. It's wet enough to do that."

Karen kept her frustration in check. Though the rope was tethered to a bench, and she could gather it for a closer look, she couldn't risk stepping into the cordoned off area and contaminating the ground before SOCO had completely examined it for evidence.

"What about recovering the body?" Karen asked, placing her hands on her hips and looking around, whilst figuring out how to get down there herself.

"For all climbing accidents and injuries incurred by walkers along this path, we call in Cleveland Mountain Rescue and a few climbing specialists. They'll be responsible for recovering the body. They turned up as we set off."

Karen made the connection as she recalled seeing two Land Rovers pull up into the car park with white and orange Battenberg stripes along their bodywork.

It's going to take forever to recover the body.

Karen walked around in a small circle whilst considering their next move. She watched as Jade took out her phone and snapped photographs of the end of the rope. Karen focused on footprints that sat heavy in the wet soil. "Okay, so there's nothing we can do about examining the scene at the moment, but have we got any details on the deceased?"

"I'm afraid not, ma'am. Normally most climbers leave their kit up here because they abseil down and climb back up. But we've had a look around and can't find anything belonging to her. Our only hope is that she's got a phone or keys on her."

"Bloody terrific. We can't go to the edge because it's too dangerous…"

"You can't, ma'am," Adams interrupted. "We've got specialist forensic officers trained for these situations and can examine the scene safely. They take all the necessary precautions and are all harnessed up for this kind of gig."

"As I was saying, we can't have a look here, but I assume we can examine the scene?" Karen continued, jabbing a finger towards the dense woodland below them.

"We can, ma'am. I'm afraid we've got another trek to get to the scene from the nearest road."

"When you say trek…?"

"Half a mile… I guess? There's a private road off the A170."

"Accessible by vehicle?" Karen asked.

Adams nodded.

"Right, let's get moving then," Karen barked as she turned on her muddied heels and stomped off back down the path, her feet slipping on the mud and leafy mulch. "What the bloody hell did I do in a former life to deserve this?" she muttered to herself.

"Karen, check this out," Jade said as she caught up.

Karen narrowed her eyes and stared at the phone whilst Jade enlarged one of the photographs she'd taken. Karen stopped and took in every detail. "Shit… Really?"

Jade shrugged. "That doesn't look like a frayed rope that's snapped. That looks like a clean cut."

14

Before leaving the visitor car park, Karen instructed other officers to make their way back towards the top of the crag and cordon off the area fifty yards in both directions. They were to begin a fingertip search for any evidence or possessions.

Karen watched members from the mountain rescue team split off into different directions, with several hauling their equipment on to a quad bike before heading towards the clifftop. The others set off for the main road and towards the base of the cliff.

At Belinda's call, Karen turned to see her being accompanied by an older stocky man with a grey beard and glasses. He walked with a slight limp, which made him wince each time he tried to walk too fast.

"Karen, this is Martin Williams, the visitor centre supervisor. We may have a name for our victim." Belinda glanced at her notepad. "Beth Hayes. A regular climber to the area."

"Ooh, aah, damn bloody knee!" Williams moaned as he waited for the pain to subside.

"You okay?" Karen asked.

Williams waved away Karen's concern with a smile. "Oh, don't mind me. Too bloody old for this stuff. Waiting for a knee replacement. Two years. Arthritis you see. The damp doesn't help," William said, poking a finger up towards the sky.

Karen continued. "Do you know the individual who's fallen... Beth Hayes?"

"I know of her. I've spoken to her a few times. Lovely, attractive young lady. Great smile, perfectly shaped teeth, small eyes, and big red cheeks that make her look like a chipmunk," William said, gripping both of his cheeks to emphasise the point.

Karen furrowed her brow, amused at the description given. From experience, most witnesses would point out features like a victim's or suspect's build, how they spoke, their dress sense, or personality.

"How can you be certain it's her?"

Williams shrugged. "I can't, to be honest. But we keep a log back at the visitor's office. We ask all climbers to enter their personal details in the log before they set off for a climb to help us in an eventuality like this. I've had diabetics collapse. Walkers keel over with chest pains, and climbers slip and break an arm or leg. It makes sense to keep a log of who's coming and going, know what I mean?" Williams stroked his beard and stared at the ground for a few moments. "Beth signed in a couple of hours ago and hasn't signed out, so I'm assuming it *could*

Left To Fall 55

be her, unless she's decided to move on and try a second climb."

"According to Mr Williams, Beth Hayes drives a grey Corsa, and the registration matches the one that's parked over there," Belinda pointed out.

Karen glanced towards the car. "Put a cordon around the vehicle for the time being until we confirm an ID."

"Yep."

"What can you tell us about Beth? Can you remember what she was wearing? What she had with her?"

Williams narrowed his eyes searching his memory. "She had a black North Face padded jacket on when she came in. That's it…" His eyes widened as his mind gave up more information. "She carried a pink rucksack. I remember her tossing her ropes on the floor before smiling and filling in the log."

Karen hadn't recalled seeing a pink rucksack in the vicinity. She made a mental note to have the officers search for one. *Perhaps it had been pushed further under one of the bushes to stop someone from nicking it?*

"Did she say anything about her climb? Or where she was heading?"

"The lass said she was going to be abseiling down Night Watch gully and then completing the ascent. If it's not Beth down there, then maybe she changed her mind at the last minute and headed off to a different location?" Williams glanced back over his shoulder towards a path he knew she would have taken.

"I won't confess to knowing anything about climbing, rock

climbing or whatever you call it. But is that safe to do on her own?" Karen asked, feeling completely out of her depth.

"Absolutely. It can be done solo or as part of a group."

"Did you notice anyone else with her, or hanging around outside?"

William shook his head.

Karen thanked him for his time before checking her phone. They had been here for over an hour already. She was desperate to see the scene but dreaded the horrors they would find.

15

Karen gave up hope of saving her shoes having trudged a second time through dense undergrowth and sodden earth to reach the base of the cliff. They had parked in a small clearing close to Gormire Lake before making the rest of the journey on foot. Though an impressive view from the top, the view from below was as breathtaking. A weathered, ragged, and grey limestone monolith erupted from the ground and appeared to swallow up the sky.

An arm and leg that hung over a small ledge wrested her gaze away from the view. A trickle of blood snaked its way to the ground.

"Why would anyone want to climb this?" Jade said, as she craned her neck to take in the monstrosity. "I wouldn't even know where to start."

Karen nodded. "Me too. It gives me the creeps just staring at it. To think it's a thin rope stopping you from falling."

"I wonder if that's what the victim thought too…"

The enormity of the task wasn't lost on Karen as the rescue team picked their way down the cliff towards the body, whilst several colleagues tackled it from the ground, placing a ladder against the ledge.

Belinda coordinated police efforts from the visitor centre and informed Karen that a specialist forensic team had arrived headed by Bart Lynch, the CSI manager. They would be coming down the cliff face to gather vital evidence in parallel to the recovery operation.

The conversation with Williams bothered Karen. He'd spoken about how climbers left their personal possessions at the top before abseiling down. However, when she had scoped the scene, there was no evidence of personal possessions, not even a water bottle.

Karen didn't envy the rescue team as they navigated the wet and slippery rock face. Yet another hour passed before they finally reached the ledge and judging from the pain and twisted features etched on their faces, a horrific sight greeted them.

"There's not much left of her," one shouted.

With no further risk of loose debris being dislodged and falling on them as a new team took on their descent, their colleagues who'd stayed on the ground could now scale the ladder to join them on the ledge.

"Any personal possessions up there?" Karen shouted.

"I'm afraid not. Well not that we can see at the moment."

"What kind of injuries has she got?"

"It's more like what injuries hasn't she got…" the rescue worker replied. He glanced back up towards the crag and back down at the victim a few times. "It looks like she's hit the rock several times on her way down. I can see at least one, if not two points of impact with the rock face. She has extensive facial injuries, and from the positioning of her body suffered multiple broken bones and probably massive internal injuries."

Karen's chest heaved. The kind of injuries being described were akin to a road traffic accident she had attended as a newly qualified constable. A cyclist had been caught under a forty-four-ton articulated lorry and dragged more than fifty yards. Her colleagues had spent hours identifying body parts strewn across the street. She would never wash from her mind the horrific image of a solitary eyeball staring back at her in the middle of a busy high street.

16

Karen watched as the remains were gently placed in a body bag and secured to a rigid cradle before being slowly lowered to the ground. It was a sombre moment not lost on the officers and rescue workers who handled the cradle with care and compassion.

By now Karen had been joined by Izzy, the gregarious Isabelle Armitage, consultant pathologist at York Hospital. Karen hadn't had much opportunity to meet her since the Bailey case, but regardless of any situation, Isabelle had a knack for taking everything in her stride. As she once put it a dead body is a dead body. Karen didn't necessarily agree with that sentiment. Each body recovered was the son, or daughter, brother, or sister, mother or father of a family. Lives would be torn apart by the news they'd lost a loved one, especially in such a tragic and horrific way.

Karen did understand Isabelle's sentiment. They were both in a line of work where they would come across the most heinous of crimes, and sometimes witness catastrophic injuries which no living human should see. To a certain extent the job hardened them and though they still carried feelings, maintaining the clinical boundary between the dead and the living was the only thing that got them through such cases.

She remembered attending a house fire many years ago as a probationer. Though the mother and two children had escaped with severe burns, the father had died tackling the blaze on his own. His charred remains were discovered in the kitchen. Karen remembered racing into the back garden to throw up. And yet the firefighters joked about how the family barbecue had gone well. At the time she'd thought of it as cold, insensitive and callous, but with experience realised it had been their coping mechanism.

"Karen, I hope this isn't gonna become a habit?" Izzy said, as she stopped beside her and whistled at the scene.

"Grim, but at least we're in the fresh air," Karen offered by way of injecting humour into the situation, before introducing Isabelle to Jade.

Izzy had come prepared, and from experience was fully kitted out with thick chunky wellington boots, a waxy Barbour jacket, and jeans. She glanced down at Karen's shoes and the mud splatters on her legs. Izzy smirked. "Hmm…"

"Don't even go there. I'm still finding my feet…" Karen fumed.

"Well, your feet certainly found something," Izzy grimaced, sniffing the air. "I'm not sure about fresh air, because it smells like you've stepped in something."

Karen glanced down and shook her head in despair. "Will this place give me a break?"

"Let's see what we've got," Isabelle began, snapping on a pair of latex gloves and unzipping the bag. "Oh dear, the poor girl is a mess." Isabelle took a few moments to examine the body. The rescue team had placed plastic bags over the victim's hands to preserve any evidence. "Yep, she's definitely dead!" Isabelle added, getting to her feet to reach for her notepad.

Karen stepped forward and gasped. The rescue team hadn't been wrong when they'd said there wasn't much left of her. The victim's face was crushed and distorted. Her bloodshot eyes stared up towards the sky, whilst her mouth gaped open, the lower jaw completely misaligned to the top by a few centimetres. There were multiple abrasions and exposed wounds where limbs had torn through skin and muscle, leaving them exposed like bony outcrops.

"Is it asking too much for your initial thoughts?" Karen asked, folding her arms across her chest.

Isabelle jotted down a few notes. "Well, put it this way, a bottle of TCP and a box of plasters wouldn't have helped the poor girl."

"That's stating the obvious."

"From my initial examination, I would say cause of death was significant trauma to the head and exsanguination. There was very little chance of surviving the fall," Isabelle commented as she stared up towards the crag. "No chance. Climbing accident?"

Karen tipped her head to one side. "We can't be certain. At

first, we thought it was, but Jade managed to get a closer look at the rope that's left at the top of the crag, and it looks as if it was clean cut."

Isabelle raised a brow. "Deliberate?"

"I think so."

17

Karen's stomach rumbled and her mouth felt parched as she made her way towards the front of the SCU floor. She'd been out all day and hadn't found the opportunity to grab a bite to eat. Her head banged and her shoulders ached. The first signs of light-headedness confirmed dehydration.

She grabbed a bottle of water and took several large gulps before calling the team to gather around her. Excitement rippled amongst them. Having only been newly formed to tackle serious crimes and homicides, they hadn't had the opportunity to get their teeth stuck into another meaty case.

"Okay, thanks for taking the time to hang around. I won't keep you long, but I wanted to recap on the events of today." Karen pinned up photographs of the victim on their incident board. Gasps rippled around the room. An officer placed a hand over her mouth and closed her eyes, hoping to erase the image from her mind. Another tutted in disbelief, whilst others whispered amongst themselves. "We now believe the victim to be Beth Hayes, twenty-nine years old from the Long Marston area. Prior to removing her body from the scene, forensics found her mobile phone and driving licence in a small pack around her waist."

Belinda nodded. "It's common practice for climbers to have at least one form of ID on them and a communication device in case of an emergency or accident."

"That's helpful to know, thanks, Bel."

"Following an examination of the scene, and pictures that Jade took," Karen pinned further images to the board, "we are now treating this as a suspicious death, possibly murder." Karen handed out further duplicates so the team could examine the images in closer detail. "As you can see, it seems as if the line has been cut deliberately. There doesn't appear to be any wear or tear or fraying to suggest that the rope already had a weakness, which then gave way when Beth least expected it. But we will wait on forensics to confirm that."

"Was there anyone else in the vicinity at the time? Or was she climbing with anyone else?" Tyler asked.

"We can't be a hundred per cent certain, Tyler. Shortly before she commenced her descent, she was with someone. I spotted footprints close to the edge. They could be recent but it's a popular spot for climbs." Karen passed around further snaps taken by Jade. "Forensics discovered several selfies on her phone taken before her descent. But here's the interesting thing, two other photographs show a reflection of another person bouncing off her sunglasses."

"I'll get on to the high-tech unit to see if they can blow up those images," Bel suggested, making a note on her pad.

Karen gave her the thumbs up. "If you can, that would be

fantastic. We need to identify the individual and see what his relationship was with Beth. Her body was pretty messed up to undertake a formal ID at the moment. So, I'm going to be visiting her parents to break the news and obtain a DNA identification."

Grabbing a marker from the whiteboard, Karen scribbled out a to-do list for her team to action. "In the meantime, I'd like you all to start focusing on building a victimology. I want a full profile that includes her social media presence, her work, bank and phone records, boyfriend, girlfriend, and medical records." Karen paused and stared at the picture of Beth smiling back at her. She showed energy and vitality in her smile, and yet there was a softness in her dark brown eyes. Karen sighed before turning to face her team. "If this was a deliberate act, which I believe it was, then she was murdered. We need to know why. Any questions?"

A sea of faces stared back at Karen. She sensed tiredness in their expressions but also a desire to crack on with the case. Every new case came with an abundance of excitement, confusion and intrigue for investigative officers, and this was no different. Notes were being taken, photos were being examined and cross-examined between the officers as motives were thrown about. *Organised chaos*, Karen often thought, but she loved it.

"Okay, team. For those clocking off, head home and get some rest. We're going to have our hands full for the coming few days. Late shift, I want any important updates or discoveries sent through to me." With that, Karen wrapped up the meeting and watched her officers filter off still deep in their own discussions.

18

Karen stood outside the address listed on Beth's driving licence with her stomach turning. Despite being in this situation many times throughout her career, it never got any easier. In her mind the police trained you to fight crime, be inquisitive, search for clues, and bring people to justice. They also taught you how to defuse heated situations. But one thing they could never teach you was the art of breaking bad news to friends and family. Yes, they told you what to say, and how to approach a situation, but they could never factor in the raw human response to being given the news.

Karen took a few deep breaths and looked around the street. A quiet residential street where the odd car passed her. Once darkness had fallen, the houses were lit up like an assortment of Christmas lights. Families carried on their normal lives behind closed doors and in the warmth. Children did their homework, dinners were prepared and workers returned home.

This family was about to have their world turned upside

down. She pushed through the garden gate and pressed the doorbell before drawing a deep breath. Her nerves tingled and her chest felt heavy.

A man answered the door and studied Karen with curiosity, pushing his glasses back up his nose. "Hello, can I help you?"

"Mr Hayes? David Hayes?"

"Yes… That's correct."

Karen held up her warrant card. "I'm DCI Karen Heath from North Yorkshire Police, may I come in for a few moments."

David's eyes narrowed beneath his bushy brows. "Can I ask what it's in connection with?"

"Do you have a daughter, Beth Hayes?"

David stiffened, worry lines etching his face. "Oh dear. Is she okay? Has she had a car accident or something?"

"I'd prefer to discuss the matter with you inside if that's okay?" Karen insisted.

David agreed, and ushered her into the front lounge, calling to his wife at the same time, who came rushing in just seconds behind him wiping her hands on a dishcloth.

Karen quickly surveyed the room and the row of photographs that lined the mantelpiece above the fireplace. Christmases, birthday parties, a university graduation, Mother's Day lunch. Laughter and smiles burst into life from each photo she scanned. Moments in a family life captured forever and now about to be shattered. Karen spotted several photographs of a young female who appeared to look similar to the picture on the driving licence recovered from the deceased.

The house had a warmth to it. Not just in the sense of warm and cosy in temperature, but in feeling too. The place felt inviting and safe. Karen's eyes lingered on the photos. She imagined Beth growing up surrounded by love and laughter. A young girl racing in after school, kicking off her shoes, tossing her school bag to one side and raiding the fridge much to her mother's consternation. Boyfriends, teenage tantrums, and piles of clothes across her bedroom floor.

Questions tumbled from their mouths, so incoherent at times that Karen struggled to make out the actual words. She calmed them both down and asked them to take a seat before she dropped on to the sofa opposite them.

Karen pulled out a clear evidence bag from her handbag. Before she could open her mouth, Carol Hayes's eyes glistened as tears began to pool in them. She thrust a hand over her mouth as her chin wobbled.

"Earlier this morning we were called to a scene where an injured female was discovered. On her person were found a mobile phone and this driving licence." Karen handed the evidence bag to Carol, who sat close to her. "Is this your daughter in the picture?"

Carol's hands shook as she held the bag. She turned it for her husband to see. His eyes widened as he gasped before nodding in reply. He tried to speak but he mouthed silent words.

Karen swallowed hard. "I'm really sorry to say that the injured female was pronounced dead at the scene. Because of the items that we found on her, and that the picture in a driving licence appears to match the pictures on your mantelpiece," Karen added, casting an eye towards the fireplace, "we believe it may be your daughter Beth Hayes, although we'll be waiting for a formal identification."

A guttural howl tore through the room.

19

Carol's head spun as a tidal wave of grief consumed her. She collapsed into her husband's arms. Karen jumped to her feet and raced towards Carol grabbing her by the shoulders to lay her down on the sofa. She asked David to fetch a glass of water whilst she opened one of the lounge windows to let in fresh air. The chill of the night whipped in through the opening, bringing instant relief to the stuffy atmosphere.

Karen waited a few moments for Carol to regain her composure. After several offers, the woman refused the offer of an ambulance.

This isn't going like I planned, but at least the woman was sitting down.

Karen sat patiently as an awkward spectator whilst David sat by his wife's side stroking her forehead and whispering words of support. Finally, Carol found the strength to sit up, though the tsunami of tears still wracked her body. She clenched a ball of soggy tissues between her hands and buried it deep in her lap. Carol stared at Karen. She looked broken.

"Can you be certain it's her?" David asked.

"As I said, these possessions were found on her, and her car was found close by. It was a climbing accident." Karen didn't want to tell them she believed a deliberate act had led to her death. Not yet anyway. She needed to probe a little more but knew how much it would crush them.

Carol shook her head. "I don't understand. She was a very good climber."

Karen didn't doubt that, but assured Carol they were fully investigating the circumstances around Beth's death. Karen prompted the couple by asking them questions about Beth to build up a better picture of their daughter.

"Beth was so passionate about her climbing. She started at a young age. Indoor climbing walls, indoor boulder climbing, that sort of thing." Carol smiled for a brief moment as her thoughts drifted back to happier times. "As a child, when it came to climbing Beth was in her own world. I lost count of the number of times she climbed the stairs on the hands and knees as if scaling the side of a huge mountain. She loves… loved taking part in amateur climbing competitions. She won a fair few too." Carol looked at her husband as tears fell again and her sobs filled the room.

David nodded and held her hand. "Carol was always worried about it being a dangerous hobby. But when Beth put her mind to something, nothing would sway her. She is… was very headstrong. A challenging but endearing quality."

Karen could see how difficult they were finding it to refer to her in the past tense.

"She fell off an indoor climbing wall when she was seventeen and broke her arm." David smiled as he stared at the carpet. "Even though Carol threatened to ban her from climbing again, that still didn't put her off. She was very much a free spirit and preferred to climb alone."

"Did she ever climb with anyone?" Karen asked.

David shrugged, his wife still unable to speak. He tossed a hand in the air. "She did take part in a few informal climbing groups which met up through Facebook, but I couldn't name any of them if that's what you're looking for."

"Do you have any other children?"

David shook his head. "We tried for many years. After two miscarriages, Carol fell pregnant with Beth. It was a very difficult pregnancy and birth. Carol lost a lot of blood and we nearly lost Beth. We decided not to try again and to enjoy the fact Beth had completed our dream of being a family…" David sniffed loudly and wiped his nose on the sleeve of his jumper, desperate to hold it together for his wife.

"We're still conducting our enquiries, but there may be a possibility her rope was tampered with."

David and Carol stared in shock. Neither of them willing to believe what they had heard as questions tripped from their lips.

"As I said, we can't be certain. But we need to explore every avenue including the possibility this was a deliberate act. Do you know of anyone she may have had a disagreement with, perhaps an argument or a falling out?"

Karen's line of questioning took the couple by surprise as they exchanged glances of confusion and horror in equal measure.

"Are you saying someone might have killed her?"

"That's a possibility that we are considering, yes."

20

Is it ever jealousy? he questioned as he peeled a slice of takeaway pizza from the box and held it up. Its drooping, limp form reminded him of a few failed sexual experiences as a teenager. The anxiety that turned his stomach and sweated his brow was often the root cause of his failures. It left him a laughing stock, his reputation preceding him wherever he went.

No, it isn't jealousy. Not sexually, anyway. He resigned himself to knowing that he was never going to enjoy a relationship. *Is it anger then? Anger at why others are able to manage it and I can't?* He'd never figured it out. Everything he tried in life ended in failure. Attempts at chatting up women. Joining clubs and societies. Being sacked from jobs. He couldn't even hold down a job delivering pizzas on a moped.

There was nothing he could be proud of. Nothing he could say he was good at. And yet he still kept ending up in situations where he would make a complete prick of himself.

Humiliated each time, he would walk away with his tail between his legs. His fragile confidence shattered once again. His self-belief, non-existent.

Maybe he was destined to be alone. Maybe that was his path in life. The one God had created for him. And each failure was God's way of reminding him to pay attention and stick to the path chosen.

Who am I kidding? he fumed, as he tossed the pizza across the room and stared at the darkened wall.

His dad had said, "Stand tall and stand proud. Don't be a pussy all your life."

His dad was hardly the shining example. A self-employed businessman who spent more time at the office fucking everything on two legs, as well as screwing over every business acquaintance that ever had the misfortune of coming across him… All for the sake of reputation and profit.

"Role models?" he growled. "That's just modern-day guru bullshit. Designed to expose vulnerabilities and exploit the weakest in society."

Something changed when he'd met her. She'd been helpful, considerate, and fun to be around. Or so he thought.

He'd been so wrong.

He pushed aside the sadness which cloaked him in a blanket of grey misery.

Something had tripped inside him.

A part of him had finally found the balls to do something about it, and it felt great.

But why does the sadness return?

Fuck off and leave me alone.

21

Shattered and aching, Karen finally stepped through the door of her apartment and kicked off her trainers. Scratched, muddy and stained, her shoes had ended up in the wastepaper basket in her office. Thankfully, she kept a spare pair of trainers under her desk, and they'd proved handy today.

A familiar face appeared around the doorway to the lounge and padded across the hallway floor to nuzzle up to her ankles. Manky purred in delight that his mummy had returned.

"Aw, you missed me, sweetie? I've missed you too. Let's get you dinner, hey?"

That appeared to be music to Manky's ears as his meows grew louder. She opened a tin of cat food and emptied it into his bowl before pulling out a bottle of wine from her fridge and pouring herself a large glass. She took a gulp and enjoyed its coolness trickle down her throat. She'd always marvelled at the effect one large gulp had on the human body. It was an instant panacea for all aches and pains, worries and fears.

A buzz on the intercom had her dashing back to the hallway to answer it. She buzzed Zac in and opened the door, waiting to greet him.

"Hello, stranger…" he said as he leant in and kissed her. "I thought you'd forgotten about me."

Karen rolled her eyes. "How could I do that? You're half of the reason I'm in bloody York."

Zac grabbed his chin and stared up towards the ceiling as if in deep thought. "Now what was it? Ah, 'I'll buzz you later on today' were the words I think you used?"

Karen laughed, closing the door behind him. "I'd like to say that I sit on my arse all day doing sweet FA but I am a busy woman you know! Besides, I need to keep you on your toes. Wine?"

Zac nodded and gratefully accepted a large glass before knocking back half of it in one go.

"Steady Eddie, you'll be pissed as a fart at this rate."

Zac placed his glass down and wrapped his arms around her. "I don't get drunk. I just get less classy and more fun."

Karen stared into Zac's eyes and saw the hunger deep within them. She leant in and kissed him hard as his hands reached for her waist, pulling her into him.

"I needed that," Karen whispered, pulling away. She saw the frustration in his face, and the growing bump in his trousers.

"Me too. I would love to stay but I need to get back.

Summer is having an evening at mine with a few school friends, but my neighbour can only watch them for a bit. The prospect of leaving four twelve-year-olds unsupervised fills me with dread. I've got visions of getting back to find the kitchen ablaze."

Zac knocked back the rest of his wine before pulling Karen in again. "I don't know if I've told you this, but I'm so glad you've moved up here."

Karen pursed her lips and smiled at him. "Yeah, you've told me a few times. I am too. A new town. A new job. And a new man. What's not to like?"

"I couldn't have put it better myself. Except the man thing. Hey, I heard about the new case. It sounds pretty gruesome. Deliberate I hear?"

"Good news travels fast then. To be honest it's great to get a really challenging case. I was a bit worried that Jade might struggle with the slower pace of life, but she's got stuck in."

"Have you got any leads?" Zac asked, fishing his car keys out of his pocket.

Karen went on to explain that it was still early days yet, but Beth's phone had revealed a potential lead that they would be following up tomorrow.

"I went to see her parents this evening. They're in a right state. Once I've got her formally ID'd I can assign them a Family Liaison Officer. Bloody heartbreaking to hear them talk about Beth. Only child as well."

Zac raised a brow and drew back his lips.

"Exactly," Karen agreed. "A fun, energetic woman who

loved the outdoors and lived for climbing. Her parents spoke about how Beth completed their dream of having a family, and now…"

"It's all snatched away."

"Life's a bitch sometimes. Listen, let's not dwell on that, I've had enough for today. You're going to be late, and I need some sleep."

"Okay, I better dash. Let me know if you need any help or advice."

"Thanks, I will do. Go on, you head off home. I'll speak to you tomorrow."

After Zac left, Karen only managed to rustle up a bowl of cornflakes and a cup of tea before grabbing a shower and crawling into bed. She had planned to do more unboxing this evening. That would have to wait for another day as she drifted off.

22

The smell of fresh coffee and warm pastries greeted Karen's senses as she breezed through the door of the SCU. There was a hive of activity with keyboards being tapped, phone conversations buzzing around the room, and officers exchanging information. A wave of pleasure flowed over her at the sight. A cohesive team who got along and worked hard. Though the unit was in its infancy she had great hopes for it. The fact that Laura had given her the opportunity to build her own team was a dream come true.

She dropped her coat and bag on Jade's desk. "Morning, did you sleep well?"

Jade nodded before thrusting her arms above her head to stretch her back. "Like… A… Baby. That was certainly a full-on first day for me. It took me by surprise a bit, but I'll get used to it."

Karen placed a reassuring hand on Jade's shoulder. "You

did fantastic, and I'm relieved that you've settled in so well."

"Karen, there's a Danish and a vanilla latte for you if you want one?" Ed shouted across the floor.

Not needing a second invitation Karen's eyes lit up as she raced across the room. "I could get used to this. What's the occasion?"

Ed laughed. "No particular occasion. Once a week we take it in turns to treat everyone to a breakfast. Today was my turn and voila, I came bearing gifts."

Karen took a massive chunk from her pastry, pushing aside the images of butter being slathered on her thighs and belly. *This isn't going to do anything for my figure!* But for some reason today she was famished. Perhaps it was because she hadn't eaten yesterday and had gone to bed on a bowl of cereal. She gathered the team for a quick catch-up, slurping her latte whilst picking off flakes of pastry caught on the front of her jumper.

Karen began by giving the team an update on her visit to Beth's family last night, including the information around Beth's passion for climbing. "We'll know this morning whether her parents are able to formally identify her body. Much depends on whether Isabelle's team has been able to make her presentable enough." Karen pulled out an evidence bag from inside her notebook. "I took Beth's toothbrush, and a few strands of hair from her pillow for DNA identification. Can someone get that across to the forensic team, please?"

A support officer stepped up to take the bag.

"I'll appoint a family liaison officer for Beth's family. What information have we been able to gather about Beth?" Karen asked, picking up a whiteboard marker in readiness to jot down a few notes.

"She was a mature student at Swansea University, having studied geography. She graduated three years ago," Ed began. "She worked as a freelance writer and blogger. Mainly around outdoor climbing but had published a few books on the subject."

That small bit of information was enough to pique Karen's interest. *Accomplished climber. Safety would be her paramount concern.*

Darren Chilvers, a support officer assigned to Karen's team, continued the theme of her being an accomplished climber. He added she had started as an indoor competition climber, before moving to outdoor climbing after meeting one of her idols in Smith Rock State Park, Oregon. "Chad Cooper was the fella. She joined him and two other climbers for their assent of the Nose of El Capitan in Yosemite, California. Read a few articles where she was interviewed about her climb, and though she considered herself an amateur climber, she scaled it in a little over three hours."

Karen shrugged; the time meant nothing to her.

Darren elaborated. "The speed record is two hours and twenty-three minutes. So she was pretty quick."

This added more weight to Karen's theories.

"It goes on," Belinda offered. "I did a bit of digging around into her background. She was well travelled, and we've found dozens of photos of her climbs in Portland Bill, Dorset, and Almscliff Crag in Yorkshire, Snowdonia,

Gogarth in Anglesey, Cheddar Gorge in Somerset, and Malham Cove in Yorkshire. She's been all over the place. And that's not including the climbs in Europe and the States."

Karen managed to scribble all of those locations to the whiteboard before taking a step back to blow out her cheeks.

Jade jotted down as much as she could, keen not to miss any details.

Belinda stood and handed out a printout she had prepared earlier. "Phone logs have been downloaded, and there were a lot of personal messages from a guy called Adam Taylor. There was a relationship of some sorts going on between them."

Karen scanned the messages and raised a brow. "Track down Adam's contact details. I think we need to have a conversation with him. Okay, let's wrap this up and get back to work. I want Beth's life turned upside down and inside out. From all accounts she was a seasoned and accomplished climber. I want to know why she fell to her death."

23

Jade grabbed a seat opposite Karen and scanned her room. "You're right about this place. Anyone would think we're sitting in an expensive solicitor's office," she tutted. "Why couldn't we have offices like this back in London?"

"It's called budget cuts, my dear. The Met is the biggest force in the UK, and under the biggest scrutiny. I don't know how they got away with building the New Scotland Yard HQ. That's like this setup."

"Yep, you've seen some of the nicks that we turn up at. Paint peeling off the walls, loos that are thirty years old, and smell like it, computers that keep breaking down, personal radios that struggle to get a decent signal, the list goes on."

"Listen to you Miss Doom and Gloom. You're not there any more; you're here. And look at what you have at your disposal," Karen said, waving her arm in a big arc in front of her. "I promise you. This is going to be great. And besides the bonus for you is that the force here is smaller."

Jade looked at her in confusion.

Karen rolled her eyes. "Oh my God, do I literally need to spell it out for you. It… means… that there's more opportunity for you to be noticed. You get more hands-on involvement, which will deepen your experience, and give you more opportunity for promotion. Don't forget that I deliberately didn't assign a DI to my team…"

Jade's jaw dropped at the realisation. "Oh, I seeee."

"You haven't met her yet, but DI Anita Mani was interested in joining our team, but she went with Zac. He also has a DS, Mark Burton, a strange bloke that I've not figured out. He's been pushing for promotion. But I asked Zac to hang on to him. It's down to you now, Jade."

"No pressure then!"

They both laughed. It felt like old times again. They may have changed forces, but the connection, partnership, and friendship remained strong.

"See, I told you it would be a good move. The setup is spot on here. And I know we'll both do really well," Karen chirped with a lightness in her voice.

"You seem a lot happier. Has it anything to do with… Zac?" Jade probed, raising a brow.

Karen tipped her head and laughed. "A bit, I guess. I think the change of scenery after everything that happened in London was a good shout. There are too many painful memories back there." Karen paused for a moment in reflection. "I guess I needed a fresh start. I didn't realise I'd come up to York and not only crack the case but meet someone I fancy."

"Sounds serious." Jade winked.

Karen shrugged as she looked at her computer screen and pushed back her chair. "Who knows? Its early days. My focus is on the job. Zac is a bit of eye candy," Karen said, hoping to downplay the relationship. It had been a long time since she'd *really* liked someone. So long that she couldn't remember. Most of her recent flings had been of the drunken variety and were measured in hours rather than days, weeks, or months.

"Eye candy? Are you sure?" Jade shot an accusatory stare in Karen's direction. "I can see it on your face. You really like him but won't admit it. You scaredy-cat. Don't pull the wool over my eyes, Karen. I know you too well. Go on, fess up!"

"Stop. I feel like I'm being interviewed under caution!" Karen laughed. "As I said, it's early days and we're seeing how it goes, but I'm hopeful things will go well." She rose to her feet and logged off from her computer. "Right. Instead of interrogating and analysing my love life, Jade, how about we put your talent to good use by having a chat with Mr Taylor?"

24

"There's no answer," Jade bellowed after ringing the doorbell several times.

Karen had walked around to the side of the semi-detached property, peering through holes in the wooden fence to catch a glimpse of what lay beyond. She could see the usual things, a patio set sitting on a small deck, a rusty barbecue that had seen better times, and a couple of bicycles leaning against one wall.

"There's nothing round the back either," Karen replied when she returned. Karen leant against the glass window and cupped her hands around her eyes to get a better view. The lounge looked modern and tidy in Karen's opinion.

Jade banged her fist on the door which led to a neighbour opening theirs, alerted by the noise.

"What's all the noise about?" the man shouted.

Karen pulled out a warrant card. "We are looking for Adam Taylor. We believe he lives here?"

"He does, love. He's working," the man replied, taking a long drag from his cigarette.

"Any idea where he might be?"

"Yeah, he's a distribution manager for a logistics company on the outskirts of town. I can give you the address if you want?"

Karen willingly accepted the details, before they jumped back in the car and made their way to a small industrial estate which took a while to find after their satnav had taken them down a single dirt track road. Just as Jade was about to give up, industrial units appeared from behind a cluster of trees.

They were given directions by a young lady at reception, who Karen thought couldn't have been older than eighteen years old. Another warehouse operative pointed them towards a small office at the back of the storage unit. Karen dodged the pallets, ladders and forklift truck as she snaked through the aisles towards the rear. Warehouse operatives watched with wry smiles when Karen's feet caught on discarded plastic strapping which wrapped around her ankles.

"For fuck's sake! That's a health and safety issue right there!" Karen yelled towards them. "I break my neck and I'll sue your arses!"

Derisory sniggers met her threat as they returned to what they were doing.

"Pricks," she muttered as she approached the office.

"Adam Taylor?" Karen asked as she stepped through the open doorway to the office.

Taylor's head flicked up from a pile of paperwork. "Erm, yeah, why?"

"I'm Detective Chief Inspector Karen Heath, and this is my colleague Detective Sergeant Jade Whiting from North Yorkshire Police. We're making enquiries into a case that we're dealing with involving Beth Hayes. We understand that you may know her?"

Taylor stiffened, his movements jittery and awkward. Karen noticed immediately.

"Well... She's only a friend. I don't know her too well. Why?"

"I'll ask the questions," Karen snapped. "Are you sure you don't know her *too* well?"

Taylor squirmed in his chair. "Yeah, as I said, I know her a bit. But that's about it. Why?"

If he says "why?" one more time, I'll shove one of those wooden pallets down his throat.

"Beth's body was found at the bottom of Whitestone Cliff yesterday morning. At the moment we're keen to speak to everyone who may have known her to build a timeline of her last known movements."

The news sent Taylor reeling back in his chair. His eyes were fixed wide in shock. Taylor got to his feet and staggered past his desk, his face two shades paler. "I need some air. I can't breathe. I need air!" he shouted as he barged past Karen and Jade.

With Karen and Jade trailing after him, once he reached the storage area he made a run for it, sprinting past his colleagues as they looked on in consternation.

"We've got a runner!" Karen yelled.

25

Karen flew into a sprint with Jade a few strides behind.

"Stop, Taylor! Don't make this any harder for yourself," Karen screamed as she reached the entrance of the warehouse and skirted left in pursuit of Taylor. Jade took a sharp right to cut him off.

Karen saw Taylor up ahead staggering, searching blindly with terror etched in his eyes. He kept glancing over his shoulder looking for a way out. He took the next corner and ran straight into Jade, their bodies colliding. Jade collapsed to the ground, clutching her face before rolling over in agony.

"Jade… Are you okay?" Karen shouted as she approached.

Jade choked on her words but pointed as if to say "get the bastard".

Taylor continued to run until he hit a tall wire fence which surrounded the small industrial estate. With nowhere to go he spun around and backed up with arms raised in surrender.

"Get on the ground. Get on the fucking ground face down."

Taylor obeyed as Karen jumped on him. She grabbed one wrist and twisted it behind his back. Taylor yelped. She secured his second hand and cuffed him before hoisting him to his feet. "That was really fucking stupid. You've gone straight to the top of my suspect list," Karen barked as she dragged him back towards the unit.

"I'm sorry. I'm sorry. I panicked."

Jade was surrounded by a few workers who were attending to her bloodied nose and cut lip.

"You okay?" Karen asked as she passed Jade and shoved Taylor back into his office. Jade nodded and gave a thumbs up before getting to her feet and joining Karen.

"You've got a lot of explaining to do, Adam Taylor," Karen barked as she shoved Taylor into his seat and glared at him. "I'll have you arrested for assaulting a police officer."

Taylor shook his head. "I'm sorry. It was an accident. I couldn't stop."

"Why don't you start by telling me the truth. What was your connection with Beth Hayes?" Karen folded her arms.

Taylor swallowed hard, his face red, hot, and sweaty. His eyes jumped around as his body jittered. "Okay. Okay. I did know Beth. I met her in a climbing group meet up. We didn't really talk to begin with until the end of my first climb. I was a bit of a newbie, and she really helped me out. We hit it off after that."

"And then, judging by your string of text messages, you got involved sexually?"

Adam nodded and buried his head in his hands. "But we kept quiet about it. We didn't want anyone to know. We'd meet in secret. Before a climb, or at a hotel, and sometimes we'd pull up in a quiet country lane, and well... you know."

"How very romantic," Karen quipped. "When was the last time you saw her?"

"A few days ago. I'd spoken to her since. In fact, I'd spoken to her first thing yesterday morning. We had a falling out."

Karen looked across to Jade who had a pile of tissues pressed against her face.

"Why the secrecy?"

Taylor groaned. "Because I have a long-term girlfriend that I live with. Beth knew about my relationship anyway," he added quickly.

"Where were you yesterday morning between seven a.m. and ten a.m.?"

"I swear I didn't have anything to do with her death. I promise on my life."

"Taylor, answer the question."

Taylor's voice faltered. "It was my girlfriend's birthday. I took her out for breakfast."

"We'll need to confirm that."

Taylor nodded. "I can do one better than that. I've still got the receipt," he said, scrambling around his desk to dig out his wallet from under a pile of papers. He searched through the pockets before retrieving the receipt in question and handing it across to Karen. Karen seized it, making a mental note to follow up later. "We also need a buccal swab from you."

"What?"

"It's a mouth swab, for DNA purposes."

"I swear, I didn't have anything to do with her death. You've got to believe me. You won't find my DNA on her. I didn't touch her."

"If that's the case, then you're in the clear. It's merely for elimination purposes. We'll be asking for swabs from everyone who came in contact with her."

"My girlfriend isn't going to find out about this, is she?" he asked, the worry lines etched deep into his forehead.

"Who knows?" Karen replied, turning to head back towards the car to obtain a swab kit. A small grin breaking on her face.

"Beth was pregnant," Taylor blurted.

Karen spun around. "What?"

Taylor nodded before lowering his eyes. "That's why we'd fallen out yesterday morning on the phone. She'd just found out she was pregnant."

"Yours?"

Taylor shrugged. "I don't know."

26

"You sure you don't need to see anyone, since we're in the perfect place for it?" Karen asked as she examined Jade's wounds.

Jade batted a hand away. "God, you're like my mum. She'd be running for the first aid box every time I tripped up as a kid!"

"I could do that too, if it helps?"

"Enough! That's just creepy."

Karen and Jade made their way through the hospital towards the mortuary, buzzing on the intercom and waiting patiently until Izzy's assistant let them in. He showed them towards a side room where they both threw on a robe and mask. Karen's features stiffened as the smell hit her. Jade shuddered as it reached her too.

"Oh my God, they've had a bad one in today," Jade said as her eyes watered. Acidic bile crept up her throat and scorched the back of her tongue.

Karen nodded as she cleared her throat and donned a mask at breakneck speed.

The familiar smells of disinfectant and air freshener did little to mask the stench that smothered them. As they walked towards the examination room, the smell intensified, and for a brief moment Karen considered turning back.

With a resolute sigh, she entered the examination room, spotting Izzy at the far end nodding her head to a random song as she examined a cadaver.

"You could have warned us!" Karen shouted as she snaked her way through the tables towards Izzy with a hand over her nose. "It bloody reeks in here." To Karen it smelt like a mixture of rotten eggs, garlic, shit and mothballs.

Izzy laughed and rolled her eyes as her assistant walked about the room liberally spraying industrial strength air freshener to break down the pungent aromas. "Sorry about that. We're used to it, so I don't notice it as much. We had a badly decomposed body in before your lady. You see, in addition to the various gases released by a dead body, it also releases about thirty different chemical compounds. It's interesting to say the least. Did you know that?"

Karen rolled her eyes, bracing herself for one of Izzy's insights that she wasn't remotely interested in at all.

"Well, Karen, skatole smells like shit, indole is more like a musty, wet, yet also a penetrating sharp-clean smell. A sort of odd combination of wet-dog, stale hot breath and moth balls all rolled into one. Even you must know from your chemistry lessons at school, that the rotten eggs smell is hydrogen sulphide."

"And the aromatic garlic smell? I doubt you're cooking up a Bolognese in the back?"

"Dimethyl disulphide and trisulphide."

Karen clicked her fingers and raised a brow in Jade's direction. "Of course, how did I miss that?" she replied with a hint of sarcasm in her tone. Karen thought Izzy and Wainwright would make the perfect couple. They could talk about corpse gasses all night over dinner. The thought raised a smile behind her mask.

"Anyway... hot off the press. I have major news for you," Izzy exclaimed.

"Beth was pregnant," Karen said as they paused beside Beth's body.

Izzy furrowed her brow. "What are you, Mystic Meg?" she asked as her shoulders sagged in disappointment.

Karen explained the recent meeting with Adam Taylor and his revelations.

"That figures then. Are you okay?" Izzy asked, tipping her head in Jade's direction, staring at her split lip and swollen nose. "We can get that looked at, if you want?"

Jade glared at Karen who burst out laughing and shrugged her shoulders. "It's only because we care."

"I've got one interfering mother already. I don't need another two, thanks very much," Jade added.

Izzy pressed the remote on her radio, raising the volume of a rock ballad playing in the background.

Karen took a moment to examine Beth's body. The familiar Y stitching confirmed that the investigation had taken place. There was a multitude of bruises, abrasions, and open wounds to her legs, arms, thighs, and torso. In fact, very few areas of her body remained unscathed following the fall.

"I can see why she didn't survive. Oh, thanks for cleaning her up for her father to formally identify her. It couldn't have been easy for him."

Izzy shook her head. "He *was* distraught. He could hardly stand by the end. Even though we told him he didn't have to go through with it, he was insistent. A brave man."

Karen nodded, agreeing with the sentiment. "What can you tell us about her?"

"Cause of death was as I expected, catastrophic trauma injuries to her head and body, and blood loss. She was about seven or eight weeks pregnant. We've taken blood samples, and nail scrapings. There was a large amount of debris beneath most of the nails with large abrasions to her fingertips."

"Such a waste." Jade sighed.

Karen made a note to follow up on that point. She wondered if it was common for climbers to pick up debris or experience damage to the fingertips whilst climbing rock surfaces.

Izzy moved around the cadaver. "Other than that, she was fit and healthy. She ate oats for breakfast and what looks like a banana. I examined and weighed all her internal organs, and there was no sign of disease."

"No signs of a weapon being used on her?"

Izzy shook her head. "Not that I saw, Karen. There didn't

appear to be any blunt force trauma injuries from something like a hammer or another metal object. There was no evidence of stab wounds either." Izzy stepped back and cast her eye up and down the body.

"All the visible injuries were sustained through her fall. If she had fallen straight down, I would have expected fewer injuries. The fact that she has multiple injuries suggests to me she hit the rock face several times during the descent."

Izzy walked over towards a metal counter and picked up a small jar. "The embryo. About ten millimetres long. Do you want it sent away for a DNA profile?"

Karen couldn't bring herself to join Izzy by the counter but nodded. She felt her stomach tighten and twist at the thought that a new life had been extinguished before it had even entered the world.

27

Back at the "camp", Karen met up with Bart Lynch, the lead CSI assigned to the case. Karen had worked with him on the Noor case, and she'd already grown to like him. On each of her visits to his desk, he'd be sporting another picture that his five-year-old daughter, Eloise, had crafted for him. A dedicated family man, Bart bubbled with pride and excitement each time he spoke about his family. His wife Amy had given birth a few months ago to baby Josh and was holding the fort back at home.

Bart was in a meeting room with another man when Karen knocked on the door and poked her head inside. Bart stopped his conversation and glanced up before waving Karen over.

"Sorry to keep you waiting, Bart. I've raced back from the PM." Karen glanced over towards a man sitting further along the table and offered him a smile.

"Oh, sorry," Bart quickly added. "Karen, I want to introduce you to Gareth Crow, a rope and textile technologist. Like you, I'm not well versed in climbing, so I thought it would be interesting for you to hear Gareth's perspective?"

Karen nodded, dropping her notebook on to the table and grabbing a chair.

Bart sifted through his paperwork. "Our initial analysis of the rope confirms that it was definitely cut with what we believe to be a sharp instrument, more than likely a knife. When we examined the cut edge under the microscope, there was a small step in the rope fibres."

Karen reviewed the paperwork and close-up images that Bart slid across the table. From the pictures taken under a high-powered lens, Karen could see the individual rope fibres, and the step Bart referred to.

"This suggests to me that it took two attempts to cut the rope completely. The first cut only went halfway through and as tension increased causing the rope to stretch, the second cut was fractionally misaligned from the first, resulting in the stepped profile that you can see in the photographs."

Karen's mind raced as she began to piece together Beth's final few moments.

"Gareth, would you mind giving us your opinion on both the rope and the cut?"

Gareth bolted upright as his face lit up. "Thanks for this opportunity to give you my professional opinion on this case. Climbing ropes have very similar properties to those used in sailing. These include high strength, abrasion resistance, and stability in the presence of water. You get synthetic and non-synthetic composition types, but most climbing ropes are made of the synthetic polyamide composition, or in layman's term a nylon rope."

"Does that make them quite strong?" Karen asked.

Gareth nodded. "Absolutely. These types of climbing rope have a certain amount of stretch which accounts for about eighty per cent of their strength. The rope was dry when recovered, which is good, as ropes lose a considerable amount of strength when wet." Gareth woke his laptop screen to check a few details before continuing. "I checked the rope from your crime scene. It was fairly new in my opinion. There's very little if any damage to the outer sheath. It's made of the same polyamide properties as the core. This means that your climber would pay constant attention to where her rope might run during her climb, and also to how and where it would load over the rock."

"And to confirm that there isn't any other damage than the cut?"

"Your climber was quite careful as far as she used a rope protector at the point where the rope came into contact with the rock. Such protectors greatly reduce the risk of rope damage. I have no doubt that she would have inspected her rope before her climb, looking for any signs of damage such as abrasions or cuts from moving over a rough surface." Gareth paused to check that Karen had understood everything so far before continuing. "Even laying rope down directly on to the ground is likely to pick up debris. It can then work its way deep into the rope and cause internal damage which may not be visible with the human eye. And as far as I can gather, and if I'm not mistaken, your climber used her rope bag as a groundsheet to stop that happening?" Gareth questioned, glancing across to Bart, who nodded in agreement.

Karen sat back in her chair and studied the evidence in front of her. "This is really helpful, Gareth. We can definitely confirm that the rope was deliberately cut, and that there was no other damage to the rope which could have put her in a dangerous situation."

"Absolutely. The rope was relatively new. Each manufacturer gives an expected lifetime for each rope. A competent climber would know to not use one that had exceeded the manufacturer's guidelines even if there were no visible signs of damage."

"Thank you, gentlemen. Gareth, your insights have been invaluable."

Someone wanted Beth Hayes dead.

28

Karen took a few moments to call Martin Williams at the visitor centre before updating Jade following her meeting with Bart. "I've got two possibilities I want us to consider. Either the person who cut this rope was a random nutjob, and if that's the case then this investigation has gone up a whole new level, or the person who did this was known to Beth."

"What about Taylor? He freaked out, and he had a motive," Jade suggested.

Karen agreed and decided he needed a closer look. "Get the team to dig deeper into climbing groups. From what I can gather the crag seems to be a popular place for climbers, and I have no doubt those climbing groups offered official and unofficial events along the whole cliff. The route Beth took was one of many. They range in terms of complexity and challenge."

"So, you will get a bunch of novices, intermediate and experienced climbers over there?"

"Exactly, Jade."

Karen reached out to Ed next. "How have you been getting on with examining the locality?"

"Pretty good, Karen. I think the problem we have is its remoteness. Other than a dirt track which runs along the cliff there are no roads leading to the crime scene, so whoever was there had made the journey on foot." Ed pulled up a detailed map of the area on one of his screens. Karen leant in over his shoulder. A whiff of aftershave tickled her nose. It was a pleasant fragrance, manly but crisp. She didn't know why, but aftershave always seem to do something to her. It seemed to stir her senses and fire up her urges. Ed wasn't her type, but if she'd smelt that on Zac, she would have ripped off his shirt by now.

Tossing the image to one side, she refocused on the screen, hoping her face hadn't blushed. Thankfully Ed hadn't looked up, still too busy looking at the screen… Thank God. *Try explaining that one, Karen. I smelt your aftershave, got turned on, and wanted a bit of action.*

"As you can see from the satellite image the main route to the crag is from the visitor centre. That would have been the most likely route, but the perp would risk being seen by other climbers."

"What other options would have been available to them?" Karen asked, tapping the screen.

"Take your pick. They could have come in from the north, but that would mean coming along the popular Cleveland Way path before descending into the woodland below and on to Gormire Lake to the west. But the path into the woodland can be boggy at this time of the year."

Karen knew exactly how it felt, having lost a good pair of shoes to the boggy ground.

"There's farmland to the east. Easy enough for someone to track along the fields and disappear into the dense tree line which skirts the clifftop. Nearest road is about a mile away."

Karen grimaced as she stared at the aerial shot. It was probably one of the most remote areas she had dealt with. A lack of witnesses, little to no traffic, and the perfect setting for a killer to stalk their victim before killing them. The perp had either been very lucky or very clever in picking their spot.

"Ed, there are way too many entry and exit points. We can't cover them all even if we want to. Can you arrange for police notices to be put up in as many locations as possible in and around the crime scene? There may be a very slim chance that someone saw or heard something. And slim is better than nothing. And whilst you're at it, I've just spoken to Martin Williams. Can you grab the visitor log and CCTV from him and work through the names on the sign-in log over the last few days? They record contact details of those heading off for a climb. It might throw up something."

Karen fast realised her method of investigation for this case would need a completely different strategy. Everything that she had been so used to relying on to help her with each case was absent in this one. She could deal with not having any eyewitnesses, but the lack of wide-scale CCTV of the scene and surrounding area pissed her off the most. Reviewing footage was such a big part of information gathering and evidence that it had become an integral part of modern-day policing. Without it, Karen felt she had been zapped back twenty years.

29

A knock on her door snapped Karen's head up. She'd been so wrapped up in paperwork and putting together a framework for her investigation that she'd lost track of time.

Zac stood there with two styrene containers, and a less than happy look on his face.

"Can't believe you stood me up?" Zac said, frustration tinged in his voice.

"Fuck. I'm so sorry. My head has been so into this case, I forgot to check my calendar and our lunch date."

"Jacket potato with cheese and beans for an early dinner." Zac placed one container on her desk before taking the seat opposite and opening the lid on his. The smell of warm food filled the air.

Karen's eyes lit up. "You didn't have to. You could have just given me a bollocking. I deserve it for letting you down."

Zac shook his head, his mouth so full of food that both cheeks bulged like a greedy squirrel whose eyes were bigger than his mouth. He swallowed hard, the food sticking in his throat. "Don't worry about it. Shit happens. Besides, I was hungry and thought you probably would be too."

"Ah, bless you. Thank you for thinking of me."

"I'm always thinking about you," he replied with a warm grin.

They both greedily stuck into their food, silence filling the room for a few moments.

"How are you getting on?" he asked, taking a hefty glug from his can of Coke.

"It's all so bloody alien. The homeless man case — I can deal with that. That's more of what I'm used to. But this climbing case is a completely different ball game. The landscape. The remoteness. The lack of bloody CCTV... Oh my God. CCTV is often the backbone of my information gathering, and I've got diddly-squat of that here. It's like I've stepped into the dark ages."

Zac laughed. "You'll hardly get CCTV in the middle of a national park where often the only thing for miles that is living will probably have four legs or wings."

"I know. I know. It's just that I'm used to it. We've got CCTV from the visitor centre, but it sounds like it's just from an old camera overlooking the inside of the entrance. It's not much, but worth a look."

"Well, you will need to rely on good old-fashioned detective work then. It's a great way of thinking outside of the box. What's the latest on Taylor? Is he a suspect?"

Karen pursed her lips and paused whilst she thought about it. "I'm not sure. He's the only one I have. He was in a relationship with the victim. The phone log suggests that she was in love with him. And there're more messages of that nature with Beth than with his own girlfriend."

"Well, who did he want more? Beth or his girlfriend? Or did he want both?"

"It's hard to tell at the moment. From what I can see he appears quite happy in his relationship with his girlfriend. Perhaps Beth was a bit on the side. Things changed when she became pregnant. It was like his perfect world had turned upside down."

Zac considered Karen's words. "I wouldn't be surprised if you pull him in for questioning once you've gone through all of Beth's digital footprint. How far away are you from completing your review?"

"We are still trying to name the faces in her gallery. A review of her text and WhatsApp messages is ongoing. The high-tech unit is attempting to recover deleted logs as we speak. So that might throw up something else."

Zac tossed his empty container in the bin and tried to hide a muffled burp behind his napkin.

"Charming," Karen said, pulling a face.

"In my defence, Karen, in Egypt burping loudly after a meal is considered good dining etiquette and shows your appreciation of the food you've just eaten."

"In case it's slipped your notice, we're not in Egypt."

Zac paused as he reached the doorway. "Remember that saying, hell hath no fury like a woman scorned?"

"Yep… And?" Karen replied, as she wondered where this was heading.

"What if Taylor rejected her? What if he said he didn't want anything to do with her or the baby? Maybe she threatened to drop him in it?" he replied, raising a brow before walking off.

30

"That looked like a cosy date," Jade teased as Karen stopped by her desk.

"I feel terrible. I was supposed to have met Zac for lunch and forgot to check my diary. Oops." Karen threw a hand over her face. "My bad."

"Oh, dear. You're already in the bad girlfriend books. You'll have to cook dinner to make it up to him."

Karen's laughter drew attention from the other officers around her. "Hey, listen. If I try to cook him a meal he'll be praying after the meal, *not* before. I use my smoke alarm as a timer."

"Oh my God, Karen. I feel sorry for the poor bloke. Takeaway it is then."

"Enough of your character assassination of my cooking skills. How are you getting on with the Noor case?"

"Good actually. The CCTV footage has been enhanced by the high-tech unit. We've identified two of the three men seen following Noor. We were also able to track back a bit further to earlier in the evening. We identified a clip where all three men were involved in a verbal altercation of some sorts with Noor. It only lasted about thirty seconds or so. Here, let me show you." Jade clicked through a few files before identifying the segment.

Karen grabbed a chair and pulled up alongside Jade. She watched an empty street scene for a few seconds before Noor came into view. Noor rummaged through rubbish bins along the street. Occasionally he would pause and open what appeared to be takeaway boxes, before helping himself to the remains. The scene tugged on her heart.

The poor man not only struggled with living on the streets without a roof over his head but also resorted to living off discarded scraps from late-night revellers. Her thoughts drifted back to the hot lunch she had just eaten. A simple pleasure she'd enjoyed, and yet for Noor it could have meant the difference between filling his empty belly or going hungry for the day.

Jade interrupted her thoughts.

"There you go," she said, jabbing at the screen. "Here come our three suspects."

Karen watched the three men come up behind Noor. Whatever they said led to Noor raising his arms by his side in protest. The exchange ramped up a notch when one of the men stepped forward and shoved Noor in the chest. They appeared to be mocking him as they circled Noor, pointing and shouting at him. Two individuals threw beer bottles at him before Noor ran off.

"What a bunch of toerags. The bloke was minding his own business," Karen muttered, tensing in frustration.

Jade pulled up the records. "Dale Charles, cautioned for threatening behaviour. Robert Maguire, two convictions for violent assault. There's enough there to give us cause for concern."

"Get a couple of officers to the last known location for both men. We definitely need to give them a tug. We'll treat both as potential eyewitnesses and suspects. We certainly know they had this run-in with him an hour before his death. However, we still need evidence to prove they carried out the attack. Good work, Jade."

31

Karen yawned as she stirred her coffee in the small kitchen along from her office. She desperately needed the morning hit of caffeine to wake up. Though she hadn't finished late, it was midnight by the time Karen crawled into bed. Rather than collapse in front of the TV with a microwave meal for one, she had decided to tackle a few of the boxes following the move. With a growing pile of unwanted things that had no use now, a trip to the local dump featured high on her list of things to do at the weekend.

She wondered why she hadn't taken the time to have a proper clear out before moving up here. But everything had been so rushed. The time between Jane's funeral and her move had only been a few weeks, or so it had felt.

Team members filtered through, waving in Karen's direction as they shuffled back and forth in between their desks and the kitchen. Karen reflected as she looked around in awe of her surroundings. Everything felt clean, crisp, and professional. She had state-of-the-art computers, desks with sleek and modern lines, and above all else a team that worked well together. A mixture of characters, personalities and experiences lent itself to creating a well-balanced team. After this case ended she would sit with each member to discuss their career aspirations, and what she could do to help facilitate that. Succession planning would be key if she wanted to keep it this way.

Karen fired up her computer and soon zipped through the messages filling her inbox. Emails from other DCIs within the force were still coming through congratulating her on her appointment. *Another thing that would never have happened in the Met. It's a dog-eat-dog world back in London*, Karen reflected.

Karen clicked on an email from the high-tech unit. So far, they had come up trumps for her with the Noor case. Karen hoped her run of good luck would continue. She scrolled through the details of the report. Her officers had put in an enhancement request for two out-of-focus photographs which showed a reflection of another person bouncing off Beth's sunglasses. Karen held her breath as she mouthed their response.

"With a high degree of certainty we can confirm that the majority of facial features in the photograph are not a match for Adam Taylor."

"Bollocks," Karen whispered, sighing.

It was a long shot she knew. The timestamp on the photographs confirmed they were taken just before Beth's descent. Karen figured it was a window of opportunity where Taylor could have been with Beth, and still given himself time to get back to take his girlfriend to breakfast.

This isn't the best start to my morning, Karen thought as she logged off and grabbed her bag and coat and grabbing Jade on her way out of the station.

32

"I don't think I've ever relied on satnav this much in years," Jade said as she scanned the surrounding traffic, making a mental note of the layout of the city as they arrived at the address.

"Well, I wasn't expecting this," Karen replied in surprise as she stared at the tall steeple of a church tower that reached for the sky.

"Me neither, but it's great when fantastic historic buildings like this are actually put to good use and not ripped down and replaced with *another* block of flats."

"Okay, eco-warrior Jade." Karen laughed as she gave Jade a gentle shove.

Jade flapped her hands. "The environment is important to us. Even more so with plastic pollution, greenhouse gases, the polar caps melting, fish levels dropping, the list goes on. Think about it, Karen. This church has probably been here for at least a hundred years and then recycled for a new purpose." Jade smiled as she stared at its architectural features, her gaze drawn to the stained-glassed windows and chamfered brickwork. "It makes so much more sense than ripping it down, damaging the surrounding land, and having dozens of construction vehicles spewing poisonous gases into the environment."

Karen couldn't argue with that and left Jade mumbling behind her as she continued on her quest to educate Karen about the importance of saving the planet. Although the repurposed church looked weathered and historic on the outside, the inside had been fully transformed into an indoor climbing centre with rock walls, boulders, and colourful climbing walls.

A woman approached them. "Can I help you two? Are you interested in joining?"

Karen held in a laugh as she imagined herself dangling from her ankles or walking funny after the harness cut into her nether regions leaving her unable to sit for a week.

Karen pulled out her warrant card. "I'm Detective Chief Inspector Karen Heath, and this is my colleague Detective Sergeant Jade Whiting. I was not expecting this when I walked in here."

"I'm Tracy Shaw, the climbing club manager. We're really proud of what we offer here. You'll find clubs like this all across the country. There's an old Victorian pumping station in London, a converted art deco cinema in Wales, and even a former Damien Hirst gallery that have all been converted into state-of-the-art facilities like ours." Tracy glanced around with a smile of contentment that lifted her features.

Karen marvelled at the structures that soared towards the ceiling. Sharp angular features created an almost futuristic look, with an array of colourful hand and foot holes, and yellow, green and blue walls that boggled the mind. Karen took a second glance when she noticed a few horizontal walls that mimicked under hanging cliffs.

"I wonder if you recognise this lady, Beth Hayes. We believe she's a member of your club? We found photographs on her Facebook page that we believe were taken here?" Karen asked, holding up a picture of Beth.

Tracy examined the picture for a brief second before nodding. "That's right. Beth is a member of our club. She probably comes once a week, maybe once a fortnight if busy. Why? Is there a problem?"

"Unfortunately, we have some bad news. Beth's body was discovered at the bottom of Whitestone Cliff two days ago. At the moment we're treating it as a suspicious death and speaking to anyone who knew her."

The news sent Tracy reeling back as she placed a hand on her chest. The colour drained from her face. Tracy shook her head in disbelief, as if doubting the news. "Oh my God, that's dreadful. I can't believe it." Tracy stared off into the distance, her mind filled with confusion, her chest heavy with sadness. "Beth was lovely."

"What can you tell us about her?" Jade asked, flipping open her notepad.

At first Tracy struggled to find her voice as her eyes welled up. "She was lovely. What can I say? She was a very good climber, very strong and incredibly enthusiastic. She loved the sport."

"How did she get on with the other members?"

"Great. Very popular, especially amongst the men. But that

was harmless. People were drawn to her. As you can see from the picture, she was beautiful. Naturally beautiful. A wonderful soul inside and out. She didn't have a bad bone in her body."

Karen pulled out another photograph from an envelope she was carrying. It featured a picture of Beth in an embrace with another man as they posed in front of a wall not too dissimilar from the one they were standing beside. "Do you recognise the man in this photograph? We're trying to track down everyone in the photos that we found on her phone."

Tracy narrowed her eyes as she studied the image, before shaking her head. "No, he doesn't look familiar. That isn't the 10 Trees Climbing Club in the background."

Karen thanked her for her time and started for the door before pausing. "Are there any other climbing clubs in York that might have these facilities?" Karen asked, nodding beyond Tracy to the colourful walls that formed the backdrop.

"You could try the Red Goat."

33

Adrenaline coursed through his veins. His skin tingled as if being pricked by a thousand needles. With nothing more than a friendly nod and a well-practised smile to other walkers, he passed small groups of climbers. They focused on the task at hand, oblivious to his presence, busy planning their descents as they organised ropes, clamps, and harnesses.

It was a huge risk returning to the scene. The police may have gone, but their notices were everywhere asking for information about the incident that took place a few days ago. He could see it in the eyes of the walkers who read them. Surprise, shock and sadness with a hint of perverse curiosity.

If they only knew.

He wondered how they'd react knowing they were feet away from the person responsible. The excitement rose in his chest as he took deep breaths to calm himself.

To anyone who passed he looked like a rambler or a

twitcher as he scanned the surroundings through his binoculars, well disguised with a rain jacket and rucksack. An Ordnance Survey map in a waterproof protective case hung from a lanyard around his neck.

He felt weird and powerful at the same time. He'd read in books that killers often returned to the scene of their crimes to watch the police carry out their investigations, or to relive the scene again. He was there for the latter. As he stood close to the spot, he imagined her face looking up at him. The look of confusion quickly replaced by terror. Her eyes wide and filled with tears. Her face pale and ghostly, knowing her fate was sealed at his hands.

Her screams tore through his mind again. Blood-curdling cries for help. The thuds. He'd never forget that final dull thud as her body hit the ground. He curled his fingers into the tender flesh of his palms. *Why am I not happy?* He should be, but sadness consumed him. He'd only done it to relieve the anger that swirled through his mind like a vicious tornado that wanted to destroy everything in its path. Yet the rage remained, consuming him and squeezing out the happiness he deserved.

He wanted to scream. A burning desire to let it out and beat the living daylights out of the next person he saw, but he wasn't here for that. He needed to confirm it had happened, and that it wasn't a warped and twisted dream his mind had concocted.

Five minutes, ten minutes, half an hour, he wasn't sure. Time flew by whilst he was rooted to the spot. He moved away from the cliff towards the tree line that skirted the path. After pushing through the bushes and overhanging branches, he moved deeper into the shrouded darkness until a small clearing appeared a few feet wide, hidden behind fallen trees and shielded from those who passed by.

His eyes glared at the spot as his fists clenched. *Here. The fucking bitch came here.* A spot he'd followed her to on many occasions. She'd thought she was alone and careful.

But she'd been so wrong.

He'd seen the clandestine and sordid sessions with her lover. She'd knelt on her hands and knees being taken roughly from behind. Her moans of pleasure had only fuelled his anger.

It had pained him to watch. He had hardened as he dreamt of taking her lover's place. But that was the worst kind of pipe dream. He was invisible to her.

Why wasn't that me?

The last look she'd given her killer wasn't one of desire, but of sheer helplessness and fear as she'd plunged to her death.

34

After such a long and arduous day, Karen tossed her keys on the desk and flopped down into her chair with a heavy sigh. She wanted nothing more than the pleasure of a soak in the bath with a cold glass of wine to soothe her aching shoulders.

"Well, that was a bit of an unproductive trip," Jade said as she kicked off her shoes to soothe her aching feet.

"Yes, and no, to be honest. At least we know she wasn't a member of the 10 Trees. We need to track down the manager of the Red Goat."

Having left the 10 Trees Climbing Club, the pair had made their way to the Red Goat Climbing Club as suggested by Tracy Shaw. Unfortunately, the club was closed, and not due to open until tomorrow morning. Karen had called the contact number on the door and left a message. That was all she could do for the time being, but it didn't stop the frustration gnawing away at her.

Building a picture of Beth Hayes was taking longer than expected. As the team picked apart her life it soon became clear she'd had a large social network, mainly consisting of other climbers, who were scattered across the globe. Anyone of them could have come in contact with her before her death and already skipped the country. The task ahead of them felt monumental.

Tyler appeared in Karen's doorway and leant against the frame. "Jade, I was looking for you."

"Well, here I am. What have you got for me?"

"We went knocking on a few doors to look for Dale Charles and Robert Maguire. We found Charles but not Maguire. Maguire hasn't been seen for a few days. According to his neighbour, Maguire tends to sofa surf, so we're going to look a bit harder."

Jade nodded. "And Charles?"

"We questioned him. He claims to know nothing about the attack. He said they were out drinking most of the evening and then went off in search of something to eat."

"What did he say about the altercation that we saw on CCTV?"

"He claims it was just a bit of harmless banter and couldn't remember much of it because he was drunk."

"That's convenient," Karen added.

Jade and Tyler both raised a brow in agreement.

"Who was the third person in the video?" Jade asked.

"Again, he claims he doesn't know. He said it was a mate

of Maguire's. He only knows the bloke's first name, Ritchie. A squaddie apparently."

"Were we able to find out where they got their food?"

"Dixie's Chicken or a kebab shop, they were too drunk to remember, but both are about a hundred yards away from where Aleem's body was discovered. It certainly puts them in the vicinity," Tyler speculated.

Karen tipped her head back and stared up at the ceiling, tapping her tongue on the roof of her mouth whilst she thought this through. "You're right, Tyler. It does put them in the vicinity. The problem is we've got no forensic evidence linking them to the victim. We only have a small piece of CCTV footage that shows them heading in the same direction as Aleem. However, the fact that there was an exchange between Aleem and these three individuals on the same night that he was killed, gives us grounds to have a word with them. Can you arrange that?"

"I'll get on to that right away," Tyler replied before disappearing.

"We can give them a grilling," Karen began, "because you never know. One of them may screw up and say something that gives us a lead. I find it too much of a coincidence that three men, two of which have cautions and charges against them, have a run-in with our victim and then get a takeaway close to where Aleem's body was found."

"I agree," Jade replied as she stood up and pulled her shoulders back. "I'm going to shoot off in a bit, but Ed gave me the details of an outreach support facility for homeless people. I'm going to stop in and have a chat with them on my way home."

Karen agreed that would be a good idea. Perhaps that kind of support service had come in contact with Aleem. After saying goodbye to Jade, Karen logged off and grabbed her bag and coat. Zac had sent her a text earlier, inviting her for dinner. She left the office, excited at the prospect.

35

Jade found the first-floor address belonging to the small outreach service down a small and narrow side street. A little sign on the door told visitors of its presence and an out-of-hours contact number.

"You must be DS Whiting?" A young man said after welcoming Jade at the door with a soft handshake. "I'm James Perrin, one of the support workers. Come on in. Can I get you a tea or coffee?"

James reminded Jade of a student type. Good-looking. Early twenties, drainpipe black jeans, white Converse trainers, Metallica sweatshirt and floppy brown hair that draped like curtains over his eyes.

"Yes, I'd love a strong cup of tea. I'm gasping," Jade replied. "Call me Jade. Thanks for seeing me this evening. Sorry it's late."

James waved away her concern. "Oh, don't worry about it. We don't *really* have strict office hours. I guess it's a bit like you in your job. We have to be flexible and offer a twenty-four-hour service. And guess which lucky fella has the night shift?" He laughed.

Jade rolled her eyes, knowing exactly how challenging it was to have such erratic hours.

James set down two mugs of steaming tea and a small plate of biscuits. Jade's eyes lit up when she spotted the Jammie Dodgers.

"My God, these are my favourite," Jade said, grabbing one without hesitation. "I've not had a Jammie Dodger in ages. I picked the right night to come here then?"

James laughed. "They're my favourite too. No one else likes them here, so I know my biscuits are safe when I'm not around. If you're ever passing and fancy another cuppa and a Jammie Dodger, you know where to come…"

"You won't keep me away if that's the case."

Jade washed down her mouthful of biscuit with a slurp of tea.

"How can I help you? I kind of got the gist of it when you called me earlier. Something to do with the case that you're dealing with?"

"Yes. We are dealing with the suspicious death of a homeless individual. And whilst the investigation is still ongoing, I wanted to find out a bit more about the homeless in York. I'm from London, and only been in York about a week. So, I hoped you'd be able to shed some light?"

"To be honest, Jade, the plight of the homeless is pretty much the same whichever town or city you go to. Crime is common, and there are always cases popping up of assaults committed against homeless individuals. They really are treated as if they're the lowest of society."

James went on to describe the kind of services that they offered and the level of homelessness in York, explaining them as an invisible society that many members of the public chose to ignore. He explained that his organisation was called up to the mortuary on average once a month to see if they could help identify another homeless person who'd died on the streets, often through substance abuse, alcohol addiction, or poor nutrition and illness.

"That's awful. You're right. It does happen up and down the country. I remember having to deal with a fair few whilst I was in uniform. Most of them were drunk or high on something. I lost count of the number of times I was called to reports of shoplifting committed by homeless individuals," Jade continued. "It's quite a desperate situation."

"It is." James nodded. "They're beaten, pissed on, and often robbed. And there's no one to protect them other than organisations like ourselves."

A comfortable silence filled the room as they enjoyed their mugs of tea, exchanging the odd smile as they worked their way through the plate of biscuits.

"Did you or any other team members ever come across a homeless individual called Aleem Noor?"

"Yes, we all know Aleem. We've helped him out with clothes, haircuts, medical aid. He doesn't speak much English, but he's a friendly soul. Through the use of an interpreter, we found out that he had escaped the fighting in Syria. His mother, father and sister were all killed in front of his eyes by rebel fighters." James fell silent for a minute as his memory tracked back to conversations he'd been privy to with Aleem. "He had nothing left and managed to escape their clutches."

Jade cradled her mug in both hands. "Aleem was sadly beaten to death."

James sat there, mouth open, the shock hitting him right between the eyes like a nine millimetre bullet. "Fuck. We reached out to him so many times recently, wanting to get him into temporary housing and off the streets. But it was so hard to track him down. We can only help people if they want to be helped."

"And he didn't want to be helped?"

James stared off into the distance. "He was scared. I guess a part of him did want the extra support. He was suspicious of authority and anything official. The mayor in his village told local fighters that Aleem and his family were against the war. The very same people who were there to protect the community sold out his family. His family were beheaded in front of the villagers. Aleem watched from a nearby rooftop."

"Shit..." Jade gasped.

"Yep. You can imagine how that affected him. It's images that get burned into your mind. Your mum and dad... but your sister too..." James shook his head in despair.

They sat in silence for a short time, both lost in thought.

"It was a trust issue?" Jade suggested.

James nodded. "We only got so far with him. Building bridges of trust didn't come easy to Aleem. It's a tragedy we didn't get to him sooner."

Jade checked the time on her phone and noted the late hour.

"James, this has been very helpful, but I need to dash now. It's been a long day and I need to get home. Thank you so much for your time… and tea and biscuits." She smiled, raising her mug.

"It's my pleasure. Sorry I kept you here so long. I tend to go on a bit…" He raised his eyebrows.

Jade waved away his concerns. "Hey, listen it was fine. I love talking too, so I'm partly to blame. I'm sure you have far more important things to do."

James shrugged and pointed to his mobile. "Well, this hasn't rung, so I would have been twiddling my thumbs and marching about the place to stop myself from falling asleep. If you're on a late shift in the future and fancy a cuppa and Jammie, you know where to pop in."

"I will do, thanks. You might regret that, or at least your biscuit drawer might." Jade laughed as she said her goodbyes and left.

36

Karen concealed the bags under her eyes, applying a bit of lippy and eyeliner before running a brush through her hair. Though she hardly wore any make-up during the day, she wanted to make the effort this evening.

"It will have to do," she said, glancing in the rear-view mirror. She'd wanted to freshen up but had settled with changing her top at work before dashing over to Zac's.

"You look nice," Zac commented as he invited her in, greeting her with a warm hug and kiss.

Karen smiled. "Thanks, you smell nice," she murmured whilst burying her head in his chest.

Zac led her through to the kitchen where he was putting the last touches to dinner. "Chicken cacciatore and rice okay for you?"

"Oh, definitely. I'm starving," Karen said as the Italian infusion of onions, herbs, tomatoes, peppers and wine swirled around her and made her stomach growl. The kitchen held a warm, homely vibe. A place that felt loved and used. It felt like the heart of the home, not just a place where people grabbed a microwave meal and disappeared off to their bedrooms.

It was another opportunity to spend the evening with Zac and Summer. She'd only been here a few times but made to feel welcome on each visit with Zac fussing over her, and Summer winding up her dad, much to Karen's amusement.

"Hi, Karen," Summer whispered as she shuffled into the kitchen, her nose twitching as she sniffed the air.

"Hi, Summer. How's your day been?"

Summer shrugged. "You know, the usual. Nothing exciting. School, homework…"

"And spending too much time on TikTok!" Zac interrupted, firing a disapproving look in her direction.

Summer rolled her eyes. "Yeah, yeah. Everyone's on it, Dad. You should have a look."

Zac waved his wooden spoon at Summer. "I don't need to know how to shuffle, or watch people give me a blow-by-blow account of what's on their dinner plate."

Zac and Summer traded blows for the next few minutes whilst Karen sat back not wishing to get caught in between them as Zac served up.

Karen savoured every mouthful. Zac was a fantastic cook in her eyes. The food was rich, warm and satisfying. Karen felt a tinge of embarrassment flash through her having never taken the time to learn how to cook. She had always wanted to buy a few cookbooks and use her time off between shifts to treat herself to something other than a microwave meal for one. But something always got in the way. Perhaps it was the prospect of eating alone that took the shine off it.

After they finished, Karen helped with clearing everything away. With Summer due back with her mum tomorrow, Karen didn't want to stay long. She knew how precious it was for Zac to spend time with his daughter, and though they'd invited her, it felt an invasion of their space. Like a typical kid, Summer grabbed a lolly from the freezer and excused herself when a friend FaceTimed her.

Karen and Zac hovered around the kitchen as he rustled up filter coffee for them. It was getting late. Time had flown by, and yet a part of her didn't want to leave. They'd shared so much laughter this evening, with Summer providing much of the entertainment. Life had been so upside down recently, but Karen welcomed the happiness that lifted her. She'd spent most of her adult life alone. Being married to the job meant she'd never cracked the whole relationship thing, settling instead for a few drunken one-night stands, and the odd fling that fizzled away a few weeks later.

She was torn from her thoughts as Zac wrapped his arms around her and kissed her deeply. She wanted the connection, physically and emotionally. His hands were firm as he held her tight, his soft lips lingering on hers. She opened her eyes to see him staring at her with warmth and fiery passion. Her heart raced as her chest heaved. She wanted more and was sure he did too as he pulled away with a smile to pour the coffee. They hadn't slept together yet. Zac was too much of a gentleman. At times like this Karen wished he wasn't, as her body tingled, desperate for a release.

37

Taking a deep breath, Karen concentrated on the forensic report for Beth Hayes. It was taking a while to focus this morning. For a change, it wasn't because of the dire lack of caffeine running through her veins, but the events of last night playing on her mind. And for a change, it felt good. She'd loved every minute of her evening, replaying the events in her mind not long after waking up. She wasn't the only one either. Zac had sent her a text this morning telling her how he couldn't wait to see her again and that he was thinking of her.

She'd felt like a soppy teenage kid whilst reading it. In the past it was "sex on the first date... or not long after". This *thing* with Zac felt alien to her. Almost old-fashioned. Whatever it was, Karen was willing to embrace it and savour every moment. It left her feeling giddy but vulnerable — a bit out of character for her. It was about taking the time to get to know someone. Creating a friendship that grew into a relationship. Building an emotional and not just a physical bond. She didn't want to admit it but felt excited at the prospect of where it could lead.

Her gaze dipped down to the report again. There was no DNA evidence under the fingernails, but particles of soil linked to the soil composition at the top of the cliff. The forensic team had identified drag marks in the soil at the very edge of the clifftop. It reinforced the opinion in Karen's mind that Beth had clawed at the surface to stop herself from falling. Karen shuddered at the thought.

Grabbing a highlighter, she read on through the report. A plaster of Paris cast had been taken of the impressions Karen had noticed in the soil close to the edge. Footprint analysis confirmed they belonged to a size ten Karrimor walking boot. A popular boot available in most outdoor pursuit shops. Karen couldn't be certain of its significance as other worn impressions were discovered in the proximity.

The report was a disturbing and hard read. Beth's body was too severely injured to confirm whether she'd been in a struggle prior to her fall. With more than fourteen separate injury sites on her body, not a single limb went unaffected. Open fractures, deep lacerations, internal bleeding, and extensive trauma to internal organs were a few of the findings from the post-mortem that sat alongside the forensic report. The back of Beth's head had been cracked open like a coconut shell despite the protective helmet she'd been wearing.

Though her father formally identified her, DNA analysis of the toothbrush and hair fibres completed the identification process. Sadness washed over Karen as she imagined the grief that must've consumed her father. Her injuries would have been covered up and makeup would have concealed most of the bruising, but nothing could hide the extensive swelling to her face.

Adam Taylor had been confirmed as the father of Beth's unborn baby. That didn't come as a surprise to Karen but raised the prospect of another interview with him.

There was still the question of her missing possessions. A PolSA search of the area hadn't recovered her missing bag. *But is it missing? Did the killer take it as a souvenir? Or did some opportunist thief steal it first?*

Karen turned her attention to the latest database updates from her team. The team hadn't thrown up anything of interest so far as they'd worked through the centre's visitor log, and the grainy CCTV offered little other than seeing Beth enter on the morning of her climb before exiting again just minutes later. They had trawled through Beth's emails to uncover expired appointments in her diary for private climbing lessons with a freelance climbing coach called Peter Campbell. As she locked her PC, Karen decided that would be her next visit.

38

The address for Peter Campbell took Karen to a small new development to the west of the city centre with a modern complex of identical-looking semis that had been shoehorned into the smallest space to maximise the developer's profit. Every property carried matching features down to the front doors, drives, and fences that boxed in their small gardens.

Karen rang the doorbell a few times before hammering with her fist when no one answered. Peering through the window, she saw a tiny functional kitchen, a common feature with smaller properties. She figured the lounge and living area were at the rear of the property. Stepping off the drive, Karen walked around to the side of the property where she heard a metallic clanking sound. The sound of music filtered through from beyond the fence line.

Karen banged the side of her fist on the fence. "Hello?"

"One second," came the reply before a gate in the fence opened up and a bearded, tanned face poked through.

Karen pulled out her warrant card. "I'm looking for Peter Campbell."

"You found him," he replied, eyeing up her warrant card with suspicion. "What have I done? Parked on double yellows?" he quipped, the attempt at humour falling flat on its face when it didn't receive the hoped-for reaction.

Karen followed him through to his rear garden where she found the source of the noise. Metres of rope were laid out in long lines across the lawn, and a pile of carabiners, spikes, and clamps sat in an untidy pile on the patio.

Peter stepped over towards it. "Sorry about the mess. I needed to sort out all my climbing equipment. I arrived back from France yesterday morning. I often chuck it in the back of my car, so the ropes get tangled up and I'm forever searching around for bits and pieces. I really must get boxes to organise these things neatly."

"I won't keep you. I'm DCI Karen Heath from North Yorkshire Police." Karen still felt odd saying that. "I'm the senior investigating officer on a suspicious death. Do you recognise the person in this picture?" Karen asked, holding up a picture of Beth Hayes.

It only took a second before Peter nodded. "Yes. That's Beth. She had a few one-to-one climbing lessons with me a while back."

"Unfortunately, her body was discovered at the bottom of Whitestone Cliff a few days ago and we're treating her death as suspicious."

"Shit. Oh my God, that's awful. Do you know what happened?"

"The investigation is still ongoing, but we believe that someone tampered with her rope just before her fall."

The news stunned Peter into silence as he ran a hand through his hair. "Fuck."

"We're contacting everyone who knew Beth. How well did you know her?"

Peter pulled a face and shrugged. "She wasn't a friend, if you know what I mean, but we got on well. She had about five or six lessons with me about six months ago. Beth wanted to sharpen her underhang skills. We probably spent around four hours climbing and practising."

"Did you see her in any other setting?"

"There's a small, informal climbing group that get together. The Acorn Climbing Club. They organise informal meet ups and climbs in Yorkshire. I had met her a few times outside of the teaching environment and these climbs."

"How would you describe Beth?" Karen asked.

"Very friendly. A big smile, very chatty, and pretty hot, to be honest." Peter winked. "I always kept it professional."

Karen narrowed her eyes and crossed her arms. "You suggesting others didn't?"

He laughed. "It's not for me to say. But she did mention being hit on a few times by one or two of the other members of the group, so stopped coming. She was never short of male attention, and it wasn't something Beth enjoyed. It was the climbing that she loved."

"Did you witness any of that?"

"No. She did mention a creepy feeling of being followed

sometimes. It kind of freaked her out. She never mentioned any names, and I didn't think much of it." Peter wagged a finger in Karen's direction. "Mind you, I remember on one climb we were at the bottom of the rock face taking a breather before starting our ascent. Beth was on the phone in what sounded like a bit of a heated argument."

"Did you hear much?"

Peter shook his head. "Not really. She walked away from the main group to carry on the call in private. But I did hear her say, 'listen to me, Adam' then she turned away."

39

Karen clung to the steering wheel, her thoughts tumbling. News of the heated conversation between Beth and Adam alarmed her. Since they'd only come across one Adam so far in their investigations, Karen assumed for the time being it was the same one. Peter's comments provided enough for Adam to be picked up for questioning.

Could Adam be that callous to murder Beth knowing she carried his child? The uncomfortable thought swirled around her mind. *He'd have to be one sadistic bastard to do that... or desperate.* Desperate situations led to many suspects committing the most heinous and shocking crimes out of pure panic, rage, or shock. It was more plausible that whoever had attacked Beth hadn't known she was pregnant which made the case even more tragic. Neither notion sat comfortably with Karen.

Though Adam was her chief suspect, she reluctantly accepted they may never find the killer. Forensic evidence took them so far, but with no CCTV or eyewitnesses, and a contacts list spread across the globe her case could stay open with the investigation being scaled back. Karen shuddered at the thought. She didn't want her new role to start this way.

Whilst she made her way back to the station, Karen pulled over to grab a coffee and then called the organiser of the Acorn Climbing Club. The woman Karen spoke to wasn't aware of Beth's death, nor the fact Beth had been on the receiving end of unwanted attention. During the conversation, Karen discovered they met once every three months in a local pub as both a social event for members to meet each other and as an opportunity to organise climbs over the next few months.

The organiser went on to explain how club members kept in touch and arranged informal meetups through a WhatsApp group. It appeared to correspond with evidence downloaded from Beth's phone. There was a history of dates, times, and places stretching back over the last few years. Each number in the WhatsApp group was being contacted by officers in Karen's team to confirm their identity and find out whether the group's members knew Beth or not.

Karen's mind raced as she weaved through the streets. Beth's life and associations were spreading out like a spider's web. With more names being added to the list on a daily basis, the team were stretched as they worked through each individual contact.

Extra support officers had been drafted in to deal with the backlog of call chasing and online searches. Most of their work would lead them up blind alleys and take up hundreds of hours, but it needed to be done. Karen had done her fair share as a DC, and it was the least favourite task for any officer.

At least the organiser of the Acorn Climbing Club had agreed to email a list of members together with the locations of where they would meet. However, she stressed though she could provide the details, some of the climbs were organised between the climbers themselves for which the club was not involved.

40

Belinda and another junior detective had driven to Adam Taylor's place of work to collect him. Taylor had protested his innocence throughout the journey to the station. Not wanting to hear any more of his whining, Belinda had placed him in a cold and functional interview room and asked Karen to join her.

Grey carpet, cream walls, and embedded fluorescent lighting did little to put Adam at ease as he sat across the table from Belinda and Karen. Whilst listening to the introductions and caution for the benefit of the tape he waived his right to legal representation. A small video camera hung from the ceiling and relayed the interview to an observation room next door.

Karen leant into the table and studied Adam for a few moments. He squirmed in his chair and wrung his hands in his lap.

"Why have you brought me in?" His eyes widened as his

nostrils flared. "I told your officer I had nothing to do with Beth's death. I was nowhere near the cliff all morning."

Karen bit her bottom lip and nodded. "That's for us to decide. We were able to confirm with the restaurant that you did attend for a late breakfast with your girlfriend."

Adam tossed his hands in the air. "Well, there you go. I couldn't have been there. You're barking up the wrong tree and wasting my time."

"We want to learn more about your relationship with Beth. Was it a relationship or fuck buddies?"

Adam's face soured. "It was more than sexual. I loved Beth and she loved me."

"But you have a long-term girlfriend. Are you suggesting that you're not in love with *her*?"

Adam swallowed hard. "Of course I love Fiona. I've been with her long enough. She's even spoken about marriage in the future." Adam sighed. "Listen, I know it sounds weird and all that. But I couldn't help it. I love Fiona and I… loved Beth. It felt different being with each of them. Beth knew I was in a relationship with Fiona. And not once did she put pressure on me to leave Fiona or ask for more."

Karen pulled out a report from her folder and scanned the contents. "I don't doubt that. But we're looking for a reason as to why someone chose to cut Beth's rope and let her fall to her death." She glanced across to Belinda, who studied Taylor's reaction. "We were able to recover deleted conversations from Beth's phone. What you're saying and what we've been able to uncover paint two very different scenarios."

Taylor cleared his throat and took a sip of water to steady his nerves.

"I quote, 'I hate not seeing you much. At times it feels like I'm the other woman and that you're more interested in being with Fiona than me.'"

"Does that sound like a woman who was accepting of the situation?" Belinda chipped in.

Taylor remained tight-lipped.

Karen continued. "Beth talked about feeling hurt and wanting more. And you replied that you couldn't give her what she wanted and felt trapped. But that didn't seem to appease Beth. She wanted you to leave Fiona. Beth wanted to be with you because it was your child."

Taylor shook his head. "It wasn't my kid. I asked her loads of times as to how she could be so certain."

"I know you asked. Eleven times to be precise over the course of several conversations. And from what I can gather from transcripts, things got pretty heated between the two of you. When she pressurised you, you told her to fuck off or else. What did you mean by that?"

Taylor shrugged. "Nothing."

"It sounds like a threat to me," Karen suggested, turning to Belinda who nodded in agreement.

"Hold on a minute. I wasn't threatening anyone. I told her to back off. She wanted more. I couldn't give any more. She was trying to trap me by claiming I was the father."

"Even though her messages said that she wasn't involved with anyone else? You sure?"

Taylor protested. "Anyone in that situation would have said the same. They're hardly going to admit to shagging someone else, are they?"

Karen retrieved the forensic report before sliding it across the table towards Adam. "DNA analysis confirmed that you were the father of the baby."

Adam's eyes widened as his jaw dropped. "No. There has to be a mistake. She said she was on the pill. No!" His voice rose with each word until he slammed the side of his fist down on the table.

"It's a ninety-nine per cent probability. You were the father. I'm suggesting to you that when you found out that Beth was pregnant, you'd finally had enough of the arguments and decided to confront her. When you realised she wasn't going to back off, you decided to do something about your problem…"

"This is bollocks. You're not stitching me up with her death."

"We have an eyewitness that claims to have overheard a heated call between you."

"Okay, I admit, things did get a bit heated in our conversations. She wasn't listening to me, but that was it. I would never hurt her."

Karen pushed on. "What size shoes do you wear?"

"Size ten. Why?"

"We recovered footprints from the scene. They belonged to a size ten Karrimor walking boot. Do you own a pair?"

"I did. My car was broken into five weeks ago and a bag of

my stuff was taken. My boots were in there. I can dig out a crime reference number if you want?"

Convenient.

Karen terminated the interview not long after with Taylor still protesting his innocence as he was released pending further enquiries. The restaurant had confirmed that Taylor was there with his girlfriend at nine thirty a.m. What they needed now was cell site and GPS data for Taylor's number to identify if he had been close to the scene before that.

41

Following Taylor's interview, Karen sat in her office, flicking from one file to another until Jade joined her.

"How did the interview go?"

"Fine. He's still claiming he didn't do it. I've sent officers to question his girlfriend to confirm his whereabouts before they went out for breakfast. He certainly had motive. Two women on the go, one wanting to marry him, and the other carrying his child."

"Do you think he did it?"

"I'm not sure, Jade. From his communications he sounded pretty pissed off about Beth's pregnancy. Beth in return wanted Taylor as a more permanent fixture in her life. If his cell site and GPS data doesn't put him in the vicinity of where Beth was climbing, then we have to assume he's not our man. Can you do me a favour and get someone to chase up his crime reference number? He's got a bloody answer for everything."

Jade turned her attention towards their other case. "Will do. I've got officers looking for Dale Charles so we can bring him in for an interview. He's not at the address they visited last time so they're out there again knocking on doors looking for him. Still no sign of Maguire either. Both are like slippery eels at the moment."

Karen tutted. "They either have something to hide or they move about too much."

Jade took a moment to update Karen on her visit to the homeless outreach service the night before. She picked through her notes and elaborated on the most important points. "One thing I did find interesting is that James confirmed that Aleem's body was found in a popular location where homeless people congregate. He said there's a lot of rivalry between them for space, the best places to sleep, their personal possessions and even food."

"If it's that popular then there should be more witnesses?"

"I agree. But you know what the homeless community is like. They're very mistrusting of anyone in authority, whether it's the police or the council. They refuse to cooperate and turn down offers of help as well. James said their team found it incredibly difficult to gain the trust of the homeless. Sometimes it took weeks, months and even years before someone would open up to them and not see them as a threat."

Karen rocked back and forth in her chair whilst listening.

"We've also had further updates from reviewing CCTV footage. Following our conversation with Dale Charles we contacted takeaways where they claimed they may have gone. We found all three suspects on CCTV belonging to a kebab shop. It confirms all three came in and ordered food.

They hung around eating outside for about twenty minutes before moving off and disappearing out of view."

"How close is that to where Aleem's body was discovered?" Karen asked.

"Around two hundred yards. It's actually on an adjoining street. They were certainly there around the time that Aleem was attacked."

Something bothered Karen about this case. They had three suspects who had been in an altercation with Aleem a short distance from where his body was found. But had the argument escalated enough for them to attack him in a drunken rage? She wasn't so sure. Other than a loose suspicion, there weren't grounds to arrest them or search their property for anything linking them to the attack. For the time being the hunt was on for the elusive Dale Charles.

"There's something that sprung to mind when I was with James yesterday. We were just chatting over a cup of tea and biscuits…"

"Chatting?" Karen questioned.

"Yeah," Jade nodded. "He'd rolled out Jammie Dodgers and a big mug of tea in support of the local constabulary," Jade laughed.

Karen's mind flashed back to her famous tea and biscuit chats with Wainwright. If there was one thing she missed, it was those moments with Wainwright. A flash of guilt saddened her. She had been here for a few weeks and hadn't called him once. Karen made a mental note to call him today.

"That sounds very cosy…" Karen teased.

Jade laughed and shook her head in disbelief. "I have to seriously question how your mind works sometimes. I was there on official police business, but yes, I admit it was both informative and nice. We shared a laugh at the end. He was telling me about his time in York, university, and life in general. I can see why he does the job. He is very good at getting you to relax."

Karen started whistling the theme tune to *Mr and Mrs*, a joke completely lost on Jade who stared back blankly.

Karen suddenly realised how huge the age gap was between her and Jade.

"Anyway…" Jade continued as she steered the conversation back to business. "Following those insights from James, maybe we are looking in the wrong place?"

42

Their conversation ebbed and flowed in different directions as Karen drove out to Whitestone Cliff again. Karen and Jade had decided to visit a few homeless haunts later the previous evening based on feedback from Jade's meeting at the outreach service, so they debriefed on that.

In the meantime, Karen parked up at the visitor centre before the pair donned wellies and set off towards Cleveland Way that skirted the crag. The day was clean and crisp with less moisture in the air than her last visit. It was still damp underfoot and her boots squelched in the mud as they trekked the short distance to the crime scene. A floral tribute of messages and bunches of flowers marked the spot where Beth had tragically lost her life. Karen took a moment to reflect whilst she read the messages.

Such a waste of a young life.

They moved off a few moments later. Karen scanned the

area before following a small path created in the undergrowth which led to an adjoining field.

"Remind me why we're standing in the middle of a farmer's field?" Jade asked as she looked around at the barren landscape. The ground had been ploughed, with deep furrowed channels scored into the earth.

Karen stuffed her hands into her jacket pockets whilst she ran through her thoughts. "When I went to see Peter, the climbing coach, he said that Beth felt like she was being watched or followed. I wanted us to have a look around to see what vantage points there were. I've not seen anything so far that would give someone enough camouflage to hide from view. Have you?"

Jade shook her head. "There is a tree line back along the path and dense undergrowth that someone could duck down into, but the place is criss-crossed with footpaths."

They returned towards the path and paused for a moment to take in the view of the national park below them. It was a rich, dense green landscape with small clusters of farm buildings and properties that popped up in the distance.

"If Beth was being watched, then the best place to catch sight of her would have been from down there," Karen suggested, pointing towards the woods that surrounded Gormire Lake. "The stalker would have an undisturbed view of her, and she would be oblivious to them."

Jade agreed as they made their way back towards the car. They passed walkers and climbers, offering them a friendly smile before arriving back at the visitor centre. As Karen was about to drive off, she spotted a car pull up at the far end of the car park and Adam Taylor exited the vehicle.

Karen tapped Jade on her thigh to get her attention. "Look who's just arrived."

"What's he doing here?" Jade asked as she watched Taylor glance around furtively before pulling the collar up on his coat and head slowly up the path they had been on.

"I don't know. I think we're about to find out," Karen said as she opened the door.

They followed at a discreet distance, allowing another group of walkers to slip in front of them. Taylor continued slowly. He stared at the ground, keen to avoid the look of those who passed by before he took a sharp right and disappeared into a glade full of ferns.

Karen exchanged a glance of curiosity with Jade as they held back for a minute before continuing to follow.

"This doesn't lead to anywhere," Jade said, keeping her voice down as they gingerly stepped through the undergrowth.

"Maybe he knows this area better than we do," Karen replied as she pushed on before it thinned out into a small clearing.

Karen saw Taylor ahead standing close to a tree and staring down at the ground. His hands were shoved in the pockets of his jeans and his shoulders were pulled forward as he tucked his arms into his sides. Karen paused and watched. He didn't move for a few minutes, his body fixed like a statue.

Until the faint sound of crying broke the silence.

Karen stepped forward. "Adam."

The presence of someone behind him and the mention of

his name made him jump. He spun on his heels, tears streaming down his face, his eyes puffy and red. He rocked from side to side as he sniffed loudly.

"What are you doing here?" she asked.

"It was here."

Karen looked confused as she glanced at Jade, who pulled a face and shrugged.

"What do you mean it was here?"

Taylor wiped his runny nose on the sleeve of his jacket. "It was here that Beth used to come. To this spot."

"You're not making sense. Why would Beth come here?"

"This is where Beth and I would come to have sex."

"And you came here today because?" Karen asked. "It seems a little strange that you've turned up at the same location days after Beth was killed."

"Because I miss her. Coming here reminds me of the moments we shared together."

Karen regarded him with suspicion. *Is he being genuine? Does he really miss her? Or is he a killer returning to the crime scene again to relive the moment?*

43

"I think we need to keep a close eye on Taylor. I want a full profile built on him and the spotlight shone on every corner of his life. I don't buy his reasons as to why he was up there," Karen said as she made her way back into the city centre.

Jade agreed. "I thought it was weird to be honest. Maybe a part of him misses what he had with Beth, and he was reliving the good times. But you have to have some bollocks to go back to the place where she died. It's a bit twisted."

Karen and Jade had questioned him at length before letting him go. He wasn't committing a crime, nor was he doing anything that posed a risk to himself or others. But Karen had left him with clear instructions not to return to the scene again whilst the investigations were ongoing.

A quick dash to McDonald's would have to do for a loo break and something to eat for the time being. Darkness had fallen and traffic had petered out to a slow trickle as they parked up down one of the side streets. The car filled with the smell of fried food, but it didn't deter either of them as they tucked into their meal to satiate their hunger.

Feeling fat and unhealthy, the pair left the warmth of their car and headed off on foot. They were following Jade's hunch that perhaps they had been looking in the wrong place and needed to reach out to the homeless community. The streets were cold and unappealing. The backstreets and alleyways were a complete contrast to the busy tourist trails that snaked across the city, painting a very different picture of York in Karen's mind. It was a part of the city that many visitors never saw, and the ones that did choose to turn a blind eye.

They stopped at the exact location where Aleem's body had been discovered. It was the back of an office block with a small rear courtyard that offered a few private parking spaces and large wheelie bins for office rubbish. In Karen's eyes it was well concealed and easy to miss if passing.

"From what we can gather this wasn't a place where Aleem slept," Jade said. "But it was one of the many routes he followed searching for food or cardboard that he could use for shelter."

They continued on foot walking up and down the side streets, stopping occasionally when they came across a homeless person. Karen held back and let Jade do the talking. She figured someone with a younger and softer face might have more chance of getting through to some individuals and appear less of a threat.

So far, their search had proved fruitless. Karen was beginning to tire. A long afternoon and evening spent walking had left her feet sore and achy. Jade had far more energy than her and kept willing Karen to push on.

They stopped by another homeless individual in an office doorway. A head poked out from the top of a dirty and smelly sleeping bag. A pair of blackened eyes peered at them. Karen couldn't tell how old the man was. His beard was long, his face grubby and dirty, his teeth blackened and broken.

"Hi there," Jade began. "We wondered if you've ever seen this man around here. His name was Aleem Noor."

The man's eyes darted between the two officers. His face twitched as he shook his head violently. "No," he growled as the smell of boozy breath flooded the surrounding air.

Karen swallowed hard, fighting the urge to look away and suck in fresh air.

"We're trying to find out what happened to him. His family is worried," Jade added. She knew it wasn't the truth but wanted to soften her reasoning for the questions in the hope the man would open up.

He shook his head again before pulling the sleeping bag over his face and disappearing from view.

Jade let out a sigh before getting to her feet and moving on. They were met with a similar response wherever they went. Each individual appeared too scared or suspicious to say anything other than to hold out a hand in the hope that a few coins might come their way.

They turned a corner to find a small huddle of homeless individuals bedded down along the side of a building. There were three men and a woman. That was all Karen could determine. Their tatty clothes, unkempt hair and dirty skin made it hard to work out their nationalities let alone their ages.

The atmosphere was tense and creepy. A cold shiver raced down Karen's spine as the four of them stared at the uninvited visitors. One man jumped up, his blanket falling to the floor. He raised his arms and yelled at them. "Fuck off. Go away."

Jade practically shit herself. She hastily retreated a few steps and raised her hands to pacify the man. Karen was already reaching into her handbag and wrapping her fingers around her extendable baton in readiness.

The other three sat in silence as the unofficial ringleader fired a volley of verbal abuse in Jade's direction, forcing her to retreat further. Karen studied the faces of the other three. A look of resignation and emptiness filled their eyes. It was as if there was nothing behind them, just a blankness. They had lost all sense of hope.

Is this how society has left them? A forgotten community cast aside and rejected, fighting for survival?

44

Not long after dropping Jade off, Karen had called it a night. Her day hadn't been as productive as hoped for. However, one thing she had learnt was how hostile it was for homeless people and how fear and mistrust boiled over into anger when confronted.

As she stepped into her hallway, Karen was bathed in warmth, which made her feel sleepy. After spending the last few hours out in the cold, it was bliss to get back to the sanctuary of her warm apartment. Manky raced up to her, purring loudly as he ran around her feet like a Tasmanian devil on speed.

"Someone is pleased to see me. How about I sort out your dinner and then we can sit on the sofa, and you can tell me all about your day?" Karen laughed as he followed her into the kitchen, purring in agreement.

First Karen flicked through every envelope of mail she'd picked up from the doormat. "Circular, flyer for a local takeaway, bank invitation to take out a loan, and my car insurance reminder. Terrific!"

Wrapped up on the sofa with a mug of tea and Manky, Karen yawned and stared at the untidy pile in the corner of the lounge and groaned at the thought of unpacking a few more boxes. *Another day.*

The only thing that appealed to her right now was a long, hot shower and within minutes welcomed the soothing cascade that flowed over her. Each jet of water invigorated and gently massaged her skin. It felt so good to wash away the grime of the day and to soothe her aching muscles. Karen leant into the stream and embraced every second. She could switch off and let herself be free. No decisions to make. No crises to deal with. No scroats to interview. She could forget about work and the horrors witnessed. In that moment Karen felt normal. Reluctantly pulling herself away from a moment of nirvana, Karen dried off before slipping on jogging bottoms and a sweatshirt.

She crawled under her duvet and grabbed her phone. Flicking through her contacts list she found the number and pressed the green dial button. It rang for what seemed like an eternity before her call was answered.

Karen smiled. "Hi, Wainwright… You missing me…?"

45

Karen felt more like herself this morning. She'd got to bed at a decent hour and calling Wainwright had left her feeling great. He'd made her smile in his own inimitable way and they'd spoken for nearly an hour. Though she hadn't admitted it on the phone, Karen missed their chats over a cuppa after each grizzly post-mortem. She'd sensed in his tone that he missed them too.

Though Wainwright had asked if she'd be visiting London at any point soon, Karen hadn't been able to promise him anything. The next time she planned a trip to the city she would spring a surprise visit on him.

With the team drifting in, Karen turned her attention towards the case notes on file. The investigation into Beth Hayes's death was slow and laborious. With a contact list as long as her arm, and many abroad, it was proving a challenge to speak to them all. Names seemed to tumble from the lips of her officers as they rifled through their notes. Karen felt their frustration after visiting climbing coaches and climbing clubs, delving into official and unofficial climbing groups on Facebook, and yet moving no further forward.

The latest notes on the system painted nothing but a picture of a woman who was well liked, competent in climbing skills, and a person who embraced the challenges in life. She scanned through a few more statements. It seemed they only had good things to say about her.

So why did someone want her dead?

All roads still led back to Adam Taylor. He was the only one who had something to gain by killing Beth, but Karen found it hard to place him at the crime scene. The thoughts of an accomplice crept into her mind. *Could that even be a possibility? Yes. Everything is a possibility.*

Karen added her own notes and observations to the system. She added key points and requests for further information or clarification for her team to action. With just a few days until the seven-day review, Laura would need an update. Karen took a break and headed for the kitchen. With a cup of black coffee in one hand Karen returned to the SCU. She paused by the incident board and studied all the information pinned to it. Karen kept reassuring herself that the remoteness of the location would hamper even the most experienced of officers.

Having a few minutes to spare, Karen had called Zac on her way home from work yesterday. As expected, the conversation had meandered from one topic to another. Karen had updated Zac on her investigation and sounded him out on her approach to see if she was missing anything. Zac had reassured her that he would have been doing exactly the same.

Karen let out a sigh as she looked at Beth's picture. There was an innocence to her. Vitality radiated from her features. So much of her life to live but yet cruelly taken away from her. An image of Beth's contorted features flashed before her eyes. She saw Beth's arms flailing — her eyes wide, gripped in fear, pleading to be saved.

Karen's chest tightened.

"She was beautiful."

Ed's voice jolted Karen from her thoughts.

"Sorry, Ed. I hadn't heard you come in."

"I'm a secret ninja in my spare time. I have magical powers. My feet hover an inch above the ground, and I can move in ghostly silence."

Karen smiled. "Well, maybe you can use your ghostly powers to help unlock our case."

Ed raised a shoulder. "Maybe I can. Did you check my notes on the system late last night?"

Karen shook her head. "I'm still going through the updates." She raised her mug. "I needed a break and a caffeine hit."

"We've managed to locate another eyewitness. The man seen in one of the photos turned out to be an acquaintance of Beth's. Dylan Capello. He's an experienced climber and probably the last person to see her before her death."

"The reflection in the sunglasses?"

Ed nodded.

"Ed, get your coat. You've pulled."

46

When Dylan Capello answered the door, his appearance took Karen aback. The man obviously hadn't been expecting an early morning wake-up call. He stood in the doorway of his ground-floor apartment, dressed in nothing more than a pair of boxer shorts.

Ed and Karen exchanged the smallest of smiles before Karen presented her warrant card and introduced them. He led them into his small lounge. With the curtains drawn, a darkened gloom only added to the claustrophobic feeling. But the oppressive ambiance didn't catch Karen's attention. A mustiness hit her first. The combination of body odour, sweat, smelly feet and stale breath drew a wince from her. Dylan went over to the window and drew back the curtains before heading to the sofa where he began to pull back a pile of discarded clothing.

In fact, it wasn't a pile of clothing as Karen had first thought but another male fast asleep, his body barely visible.

"Joel, man. Get up will you? I need the room. Fuck off to the kitchen and make yourself breakfast, you lazy shit," Dylan said, punching the man playfully.

It took a few attempts to stir Joel before he begrudgingly dragged his tired body from the sofa, barely acknowledging the visitors. His heavy footsteps thundered down the hallway towards the rear of the apartment.

"Sorry about that. My mate was crashing for the night." Dylan dropped into the newly vacated space and yawned. "Can I get you something to drink? Coffee, water, Red Bull, beer…?"

Karen declined the offer as she watched Dylan. He seemed perfectly happy to sit there in a small piece of underwear that offered little privacy. But the rest of his body attracted even more of her attention. Intricate tattoos completely covered his upper torso. Karen struggled to see a bare bit of flesh. Both arms had full sleeve tattoos. It was hard for her to make out an individual tattoo as they merged into one another. A skull, fingers, sunrise, and a black bear were the only discernible ones that she could pick out from a distance. His hair was just as intriguing. The images on Beth's phone hadn't highlighted the fact that he had long brown dreads that were pulled back into a ponytail.

"What can I do for you?"

"I'm the SIO dealing with the death of Beth Hayes."

Dylan tutted and shook his head. "Ah, man. I heard about that. I won't lie; I was proper shocked. Like what the fuck!"

"We examined Beth's phone and identified several photographs which we now believe are you hugging Beth.

But we also noticed one photograph taken before her last descent, and your image appears in a reflection of a selfie that she took."

If Dylan had something to hide, then he was a great actor as he nodded calmly in Karen's direction.

"Yeah. That's the freaky thing. I saw her as she was getting ready for her climb. She was getting all her gear sorted."

"And what were you doing there?"

"I'd finished a quick climb. I like to get mine done early before the crowds turn up. I was walking back when I saw Beth. We chatted for a bit, had a bit of a laugh, and then I left her to it."

"And where did you go after that?"

Dylan scratched his stubbly chin and yawned. "Just back to the visitor centre. I had breakfast and sat chatting with Martin for about an hour, possibly longer. Then I came back here and popped down the road to get a few bits for the fridge and then cleaned my kit."

Karen nodded as Ed made notes. "Can anyone vouch for you whilst you were here?"

"Ha, man. Now you're asking." Dylan glanced around the room as he cranked his mind into gear. His eyes widened and he clicked his fingers. "Yeah. I was on WhatsApp video with a climbing buddy in South Africa. He was calling me from the top of Table Mountain in Cape Town. Have you been?"

Karen shook her head.

"Mate, you got to check it out. The views are off the charts."

Karen asked for the details and made a mental note to check his alibi later.

"What was your relationship with Beth?" Ed asked as Karen walked over to the window and glanced outside.

Dylan flapped his arms. "Nothing, man. We were friends. We'd cross paths on a few climbs here and there. The climbing family is a big, big family. Everyone is there to help each other. We talk about climbing, we live for climbing, we travel for climbing. It's what makes us tick. If you read up on Beth, then you know she's climbed everywhere."

"There was nothing physical between you?" Ed probed.

Dylan burst out laughing.

"What's so funny?" Karen asked as she returned to Ed's side.

"She's not my type. I'm bi, but she's not my type. I'm attracted to body piercings and big tats," Dylan pointed out as he jabbed his heavily tattooed chest.

47

Karen and Ed returned to the office to the news that Dale Charles had been tracked down and brought in for questioning.

Before they'd left him, Dylan had confirmed that he'd not seen or heard anything suspicious before leaving Beth to start her descent. When pushed he'd finally admitted that they'd flirted on occasion, but she hadn't been interested in taking it any further, and with her not being his type, he hadn't pursued it either. It was harmless fun in his eyes.

"Ma'am, have you got a minute?" Karen asked, tapping softly on Laura's open door.

Superintendent Laura Kelly waved her in and pointed towards the empty chair. "Bear with me a minute," she muttered, running her finger along a paragraph she was reviewing whilst silently repeating the words to herself.

Karen curiously eyed up photo frames on the bookshelf to her left. There were various certificates as well as a handful of commendations given to her by the chief constable. A large photograph of Laura standing in between the chief constable and the Home Secretary took pride of place on the middle shelf. Karen imagined it had been positioned at head height for the benefit of anyone who walked into her office. Karen smiled inwardly. All Laura needed to do was put bunting and flashing lights around the photograph with a large neon sign above it saying "look at me".

"Sorry to keep you waiting, Karen. How are things going?"

Karen really wanted to say that the case was dragging its heels. With little progress, even fewer leads, and zero eyewitnesses, the case was getting stuck in the mud. "We are making good progress, ma'am. It's a challenging case because of the complex network of contacts Beth had."

Karen went on to explain a bit more about the climbing fraternity and a network of contacts stretching across the globe. She also spoke at length about Beth's pregnancy and relationship with Adam Taylor.

"Are you suggesting that it's going to be hard to find the person responsible?"

Laura's clipped tone cut through Karen.

"Hopefully not but it is a possibility we have to consider, ma'am. I won't lie, it's going to be tough. We've little evidence to go on, no eyewitnesses to the murder, and no DNA or CCTV. We've returned from interviewing an individual who was more than likely the last person to see Beth alive. We're checking his alibi at the moment, and I've instructed the team to do a full search on Dylan Capello."

"Potential suspect?"

Karen grimaced. "There didn't appear to be anything

between them. He says he's bisexual and Beth wasn't his type."

"We don't always have a *type*, so he may have been saying that to cover up. You'd be surprised who people are attracted to," Laura added as she checked her computer screen and stood up.

Karen didn't know how to take that. It sounded like an odd response.

"I need to dash off to a meeting to review this policy document. I'm already late," Laura said, waving a wad of paper in her hands.

"Of course, ma'am. I've an eyewitness interview to do now anyway. I'll get back to the team and update you as the investigation proceeds."

Laura smiled, but it was the kind of dead smile that had nothing behind it. Karen strode off down the corridor and disappeared through the glass doors, throwing a final glance back over her shoulder to see Laura standing in her doorway studying her.

Karen felt the first tinge of unease but reassured herself it was a silly case of paranoia. She'd spent so much of her recent career being scrutinised by senior management that it felt like she was always in their spotlight.

48

Dale Charles cut an aggressive figure as Karen walked into the room. He glared at her through steely eyes as the muscles in his jaw tensed. His hands were wrapped tightly in a ball, the tips of his fingers turning white as they pressed into the back of his hands.

Karen pulled Jade into the interview with her. A brief glance at his Facebook profile showed his displeasure of women with lots of images and cartoon depictions of women being the weaker sex. She was sure it would rile him to see two women conducting the interview.

Jade cautioned him and did the introductions for the benefit of the tape. Dale waived his right to legal representation, another act of defiance in Karen's eyes.

"Dale, you seem to be a hard man to track down. Was it deliberate on your part?"

Dale sniggered. "Well, I wanted to keep you on your toes. I heard you were looking for me. I thought I'd make it a little harder for you."

"You know why you're here. We're continuing our investigations into the death of Aleem Noor. We know that you, Maguire, and another had an altercation with Aleem before his death. What was that about?"

"Nothing. We were taking the piss out of him. He was rummaging through the bins for food. We wound him up about it. The fucking idiot could hardly string a sentence together. Wankers like that shouldn't even be in our country," Dale snarled.

Karen let the comment slide, not wanting to rise to his ignorance.

"You were seen pushing him around."

"So?" Dale shrugged.

"Within the space of an hour or two he was found beaten to death. You and your friends were less than two hundred yards away in an adjoining street. Did you go back and attack him?"

"No comment."

"I put it to you that you had something to eat and then came across Aleem again. Another altercation took place and this time you took things further. You beat him so badly that he died from his injuries."

Dale growled. "You're talking bollocks. We had nothing to do with that filthy piece of shit. He needs to be stuck on a boat and sent back with the rest of the foreign scroungers."

"Is that how you see them? Refugees who escape persecution, violence, war and poverty. People who are so desperate that they come to a foreign country in the hope of living a life in peace and safety."

Dale didn't answer but glared at Karen without blinking. The cold silence filled the room as Karen deliberately stopped questioning Dale to see how he would react. He remained a cool customer unfazed by Karen's mind games as he tipped back into his chair and rocked back and forth.

Karen continued to press him but was met with a wall of silence for much of the interview. Having enough of the games, Karen needed to ramp up the pressure.

"Dale Charles, we'll be taking a mouth swab from you for DNA purposes. At the moment, you're still under caution but not arrest. A partial footprint was discovered on the side of Aleem's face. We'll be seizing your shoes, as well as any others that you own. Officers will go with you to where you're staying at the moment to retrieve those items for forensic analysis."

Karen arranged for an officer to escort Dale from the interview room whilst she headed back to the SCU. "This is so bloody frustrating," Karen said.

Jade agreed. "Everything is circumstantial. Yes, they had a run-in with him, but we can't place Dale or the others close enough to where Aleem was found. Without CCTV, forensics or witnesses, we're stuffed."

Karen agreed. Dale was too cool for her liking. He either had nothing to hide or he'd already destroyed any evidence linking him to the crime.

49

An emptiness filled his life, lingering there for as long as he could remember. Overweight and socially inept, his life had been anything but happy. School had been a challenge, bullying and mickey-taking a daily occurrence. Boys didn't want to be his friends, and girls didn't fancy him. A solitary life of being unpopular and unloved followed him around like a darkened identity.

Determined to do something about it, he'd started to exercise in his teens and soon lost most of his puppy fat. But the stigma of being the fat smelly schoolboy clung to him. Nevertheless, he still pushed on. He'd spend hours walking through forests, public footpaths, and the national park with just his phone, music and headphones for company.

He'd met a few equally socially uncomfortable women along the way as he'd navigated through life. The conversations were clumsy, the attempts at dating were tragic and laughable.

Why did life have to be such a challenge? The world could be so cruel. He wanted to be liked... and loved.

Nothing had gone right for him. The great outdoors was his saviour. Whilst out walking no one could judge him. No one could take the piss out of him. He was free.

He'd stopped so many times to watch people gathering at the base of cliffs and large boulders. He'd often hear them before he saw them, their laughs and shouts carrying for what felt like miles. They looked happy and adventurous. Living life to the max.

Watching was an obsession. He could escape and imagine that he was up there. He was one of them. His eyes would follow the path on their ascents. He pictured it through their eyes, navigating the crevices and cracks.

At first he'd kept his distance, but on each occasion he'd become braver and had inched closer to them until they'd noticed him. For once no one was judging him. They'd welcomed him like a lost friend. They'd shared their stories, the exhilaration and adrenaline clear as words had tumbled from their mouths.

On one such occasion he'd seen her. Others had called her Beth. She was beautiful. Her smile had leapt across the open space between them and touched his heart. She'd sounded kind and caring, her words encouraging him to try something new.

Every cell of his being had screamed to not make a fool of himself again. He'd lost count of the number of clubs and societies he'd joined to fit in before being exposed as a fraud. A man so pathetic that he struggled to hold a conversation for more than a minute. Humiliation and embarrassment followed him from place to place.

Something had to change. Something did change, and it had come down to Beth. She'd encouraged him to join one of the many climbing clubs. Her words had spoken about the opportunity to learn in a safe and non-judgemental environment. What a mistake. It was Beth's fault, and that was why she'd had to die.

50

Karen had barely got her seat warm when Jade poked her head in the office door with a look of consternation on her face.

"Karen, I think you need to come and see this. I had a call from the desk sergeant who has an unusual visitor in reception."

"Unusual?" Karen repeated. "Alien? As in not human? Or a kid?"

Jade laughed. "Come and have a look. It's to do with Aleem's case."

Karen followed Jade towards main reception where Jade darted off to the right and into a small interview room. The desk sergeant shot Karen a look of confusion and surprise as he shrugged a shoulder and returned to what he was doing.

Karen wasn't sure what shocked her the most. The overpowering stench of sweat and staleness, or the dishevelled woman who sat at the desk, a walking stick and several carrier bags tied with string left on the floor by her side.

Clearing her throat, Karen pulled out a chair and sat down alongside Jade.

"This is Detective Chief Inspector Karen Heath that I told you about a few minutes ago. I think you should tell her what you've told me."

The woman looked to be in her forties. She appeared in need of a good bath and tidy up. Her matted, dirty hair framed a weathered, grubby, worn face. Her crooked teeth were brown and stained. She wore several layers to keep the cold out.

The woman gripped a cup a tea as if it was her prized possession. "I saw you yesterday. You came asking questions."

Karen slowly nodded as the penny dropped. She was the woman they'd spotted sitting with three other men in a small huddle. "We did. We weren't exactly warmly welcomed."

The woman offered a small smile. "Yeah, sorry about that. Eddie can be a grumpy sod. He likes keeping himself to himself. He's ex-forces, PTSD. He thought you were the insurgency coming to get him. It's hard for him to process anything these days. Shit nightmares, terror sweats, and violent outbursts."

"Okay. I understand from my colleague Jade that you have information for us?"

The woman nodded. "I knew Aleem. He didn't say much,

but he was a troubled soul. He needed help but was too scared to ask for it. He was worried they would send him back. I think I know who attacked Aleem."

Karen was all ears now as she straightened up and sat forward. "Go on."

The woman coughed; her breath so foul that Karen had to look down for a moment to shield her face from the worst of it. *Where's a bloody face mask when you need it?*

"He ain't got a proper name, but a few people call him Spiky. He's not a nice bloke. Vicious. Been on the streets for most of his life. He nicks from others to get by. I don't know where his pit is, but I've seen him around a few times. Spiky argued with Aleem on the day he died. Spiky took a swing at him and managed to take Aleem's rucksack filled with his personal possessions."

"Then what happened?"

"Aleem went down. He's not a fighter. Spiky had already run off before Aleem could get up. I remember Aleem telling me that he would find him and get his stuff back. The poor man was in tears. He said the rucksack had pictures of his family and a few precious items he had managed to grab before fleeing for his life."

Karen recalled that none of Aleem's belongings had been discovered at the scene.

"Can you give us a description?" Jade asked.

"A big bloke. Nearly six feet, heavy. Wears a bright red Adidas jacket and has a massive scar down his face from ear to mouth. Hit by shrapnel. You can't miss him."

Karen thanked the woman who declined the offer of a lift back. The repercussions of being seen with the police were too risky in her opinion. Excited with this breakthrough, Karen dashed to the control room. All patrols were alerted to be on the lookout for Spiky, the potential suspect.

51

Karen felt a renewed energy as she entered the SCU. Aleem's case had been dragging for a while with very few leads or breaks. They now had a credible witness who had seen the altercation between Aleem and another person. Not only that, but Karen figured she may have stumbled on the motive for his killing. If it was true that Aleem's possessions had been stolen by Spiky, there would have been a valid reason for another fight which had sadly led to Aleem's death.

Karen also considered that the new information might mean Dale Charles and his friends were not responsible.

Jade updated the information on the incident board for Aleem's case whilst other officers began the search for Spiky. Initial searches on the PNC had already thrown up his details with markers against his name for violent assault, intimidation, and offensive language. They could now put a face to the name.

"Karen," Tyler called out as he weaved through the desks

flapping a printout in his hand. "Beth had blocked five people from viewing her Facebook profile. We don't know the reason behind her blocking them, but I've checked the names." Tyler handed the printout to Karen and walked through the details. "One woman is based in Plymouth. This man is based in Africa, another is based in the US. We have Heidi Moreno, a local. She's got pictures of climbing on her profile. The last individual is Gary Cowan. He has nothing on his profile related to climbing."

For the time being, Karen wanted to focus locally and dismissed the three based in Plymouth, Africa and the US. She thanked Tyler before reaching for the nearest desk phone and dialling Peter Campbell.

"Peter, it's DCI Karen Heath here. I wondered if I could run a few names past you?"

"Ah, good to hear from you. Of course. Is this to do with Beth's case?"

Karen confirmed it was before continuing. "Did you ever come across Heidi Moreno or Gary Cowan?"

There was silence for a few moments.

"Peter, are you still there?"

"Um, yes, sorry. I was racking my brains. Heidi, I do remember vaguely. She's a good climber, but very competitive. A bit of a tomboy but wouldn't say boo to a goose. Cowan, I do remember more clearly. I was doing a bit of freelance work outdoors and I remember Cowan attending a group class with me. A complete introvert. Didn't say a word. In fact he hardly smiled."

"How many times did he attend the classes?"

"Oh, just the once."

"Is that common?" Karen asked.

"It can be. You get attendees who join and soon realise it's not for them or they're not good at it. We have others who try different classes and coaches before deciding who they are most comfortable with."

"What can you tell us about Gary Cowan then?"

"Gary fell into the camp of not being very good at it. He tried but ultimately failed in a *bloody* big way. He couldn't get the hang of it and froze to the point where he nearly wet himself. Let me grab my notebook and give you a call back," Peter replied before hanging up.

52

Whilst Karen waited for Peter, a quick search on Facebook found that Beth and Gary Cowan were both connected to the same climbing clubs and Facebook groups. Another search of Facebook users also confirmed that Adam Taylor also liked the same groups.

The phone rang.

"DCI, it's Peter here. I found what I was looking for and you'll be quite interested in this."

Karen dropped into the nearest chair and grabbed a pen and paper.

"He was in one of my classes a while back. I had the briefest of conversations with him when he first joined. As part of my record-keeping, I log contact details and found he lived in quite a remote place which was off the grid. On the first day we covered the basics. I taught the group about ropes, a few basic knots, and the type of equipment they would need to buy if they were serious about climbing.

However, like most first-timers, they're itching to have a go. After getting kitted up, I let them experience a taste of climbing which normally leaves them buzzing at the end of the day."

"And Cowan?"

"He was the last to go up. He hovered towards the back of the group. And at one point I thought he was gonna give up without even trying. Every time I asked who was next, he'd take a step back whilst the others pushed forward. The climb isn't taxing or anything spectacular. It's a simple twenty-foot climb to ease them in as first-timers. Finally, when it was Cowan's turn, he was shaking like a leaf. I checked to make sure he was still happy to go, and he nodded, so I let him have a crack at it." Peter let out a laugh as the memory flooded back.

"Cowan got up about ten feet, may be a little more and froze. I mean, he went rigid as a board. He couldn't go up nor down."

"Has that happened before with any of your students?"

"Not to that extent. It does happen. I had to go up there and come down with him. I told him it's first-time nerves, and to have a go again which he did, but the same thing happened. His face turned bright red. He was so embarrassed that he couldn't even look me in the eye. I think it was made worse by the fact that there were another half a dozen people watching. In the end I told him not to worry about it and we'd try again later but he said he couldn't go through with it."

"There was no sign of anger or trouble?"

"No. Cowan sticks out in my mind because after that one

occasion, I still saw him a few times around the place. I'd be in the same spot running beginners' classes and see him standing in the distance watching people climb. I remember I once waved at him, and he turned and walked off quickly into the trees."

"And you say he just froze?"

"Yeah. I know it happens but we're only talking of about ten or twelve feet up and he was fully harnessed. I've seen people get scared, and it's natural because you are doing something that is so different and exhilarating, but he was out of his mind with fear. His pupils were dilated, and he was sucking in air at a rate of knots. He was going into full-blown panic mode."

53

Karen tried to join the dots whilst listening to Peter. She needed to know more about Cowan and scrolled through his Facebook feed. She couldn't see much. A few reshares of random photographs, and his friends list of less than fifty people. She wondered how many were *actually* friends rather than virtual ones?

"You said he lives off the grid. What do you mean?"

"I can't put my finger on it, but I sense he's a bit of a recluse. Socially introverted. He isn't married, didn't offer a next of kin contact, nor talk about other friends. Looking at his Facebook profile will confirm that. He mentioned being interested in climbing and hoped to meet new people. He said he wanted to try something different."

"Did he appear odd to you?"

"A bit. To be honest he had me freaked out by the time I finally got him down. He was there in body but not in mind. I couldn't get through to him. Face white as a sheet, vacant eyes, and he looked shell-shocked. I've *never* had any student react that badly."

"Did you try to find out a bit more about his background?" Karen asked.

"I tried to dig a bit deeper, but he wasn't big on details. I always try to understand why people want to start rock climbing. If I understand them better, I'm able to cater to their personality in the way in which I teach them. But Cowan isn't a big talker. He's a bit cold… distant. I got the impression that he watched others do something that he wasn't able to do himself, do you know what I mean?"

"Was he ever around when you were with Beth?" Karen probed.

A pause.

"Yes… Yes! Come to think of it I saw him around a few times when I worked with Beth. I didn't put two and two together until this conversation."

"Did Beth ever mention his name?"

"Not to me."

Karen asked for the address and jotted it down. She tapped into Google and clicked on Maps whilst listening to Peter finish.

After hanging up, a quick call to Adam Taylor confirmed Beth had confided in him too that she'd thought someone had been watching her from afar. Though she hadn't been certain or seen the person's face, he'd reminded her of someone she'd met in an informal climbing group. The description loosely resembled the picture on the screen in front of Karen.

54

"Penny for your thoughts?"

Karen looked up to see Zac standing in front of her. She'd been so deep in thought she'd not heard him enter.

"Sorry, I was away with the fairies."

"No worries. I'm heading out on enquiries and then home straight from there. Are you still coming tonight?"

Karen smiled. "Definitely. I know we've not spent much time together but I'm a bit bogged down with work and trying to sort out the apartment. Besides, I have a choice between either a lovely meal cooked by your capable hands, or a Tesco's microwave meal..." Karen used her hands as weighing scales contemplating the tough decision she faced.

"Oh, don't worry. I'll sort you out."

"I'll hold you to that..." Karen replied, fixing him with her best sultry stare, even though she knew she was crap with dropping hints.

Zac asked about the investigation into Beth's murder. Karen explained that their number one suspect, Adam Taylor, had been ruled out of the equation. The GPS and cell site data Karen had requested on Taylor's phone had confirmed he was nowhere near Beth's location but was near to her home. Taylor's girlfriend, Fiona, had also confirmed that Taylor had popped out to get petrol first thing in the morning. CCTV footage from the petrol station had corroborated his trip.

But the bad news had been lifted by the promising new lead provided by Peter.

"Any idea on the motive?" Zac asked.

"Not a sausage at the moment. It could be a random nutjob. It might be someone who hated her, or an obsessed ex-lover. I'm open to suggestions."

"Karen, sorry to disturb you," Jade said as she stepped into the office. Jade glanced towards Zac, "Sir."

"No sir needed. Just Zac," he replied.

Jade cleared her throat, slightly uncomfortable with the informality. "I wanted to update you on the forensic search of Dale Charles's clothing. Officers retrieved several items but couldn't find the coat he was wearing. The chances are he's got rid of it or left it at someone else's property. But we'll keep looking."

It wasn't news Karen wanted to hear, but with each passing day, Dale Charles became less of a suspect.

"We have officers visiting all the local haunts of where the homeless hangout or sleep. There have been no sightings of Spiky so far."

"Okay. Thanks, Jade."

"I hope Karen's helping you to settle in? Is she looking after you?" His eyes shifted between Jade and Karen. "Or she'll have to answer to me."

Jade pulled a face of feigned helplessness. "I'd love to say she has but every time I've asked, Karen's been too busy."

"Karen…" Zac said slowly as he turned towards her.

Karen's eyes widened as her jaw dropped. "You cheeky cow. You're trying to get me in trouble."

"Don't believe anything she says. She is no Mother Theresa." Jade winked in Karen's direction.

"We'll have words later, Karen," Zac said as he walked off, wagging a finger in her direction.

Once he'd disappeared from sight, Jade couldn't contain her laughter any longer. "I can see why you like him. He's nice."

"Oi, keep your mitts off him. He's mine."

"You can have him. He's too old for me. I like him. He'll be good for you. I reckon he'll calm that reckless streak in you. Don't think I didn't see you staring at him all gooey-eyed whilst he was talking to me."

A red flush filled Karen's cheeks.

55

After a quick catch-up with the team, Karen sent most of them home for an early evening. An email on her desktop laid out the details of Taylor's crime reference report. His car had been broken into whilst he'd been shopping. The vehicle crime appeared opportunistic with the usual things being stolen. Karen read the list. Karrimor boots, Ray-Ban sunglasses, a coffee flask, a few pound coins, and a Karrimor jacket. Karen let out a sigh.

Not wanting to be late in getting to Zac's, Karen dashed home for a quick shower and change of clothes.

Driving over to Zac's, her mind was filled with excitement and apprehension. They hadn't spent much time alone, but Karen looked forward to getting Zac on his own. There was a comfortable ease between them. They got on professionally, they liked similar things, and they laughed a lot. These simple things had been missing in nearly all of her *relationships*. Perhaps it was why being with Zac felt different.

She rang the doorbell but was taken by surprise when Summer answered. Her face lit up on seeing Karen.

"Hi, Karen. Come in. Dad is in the kitchen finishing off dinner. He is taking ageeees!" Summer moaned, her voice rising to make sure Zac heard.

"Lovely to see you, chicken. How have you been? Are you not going to Mum's?"

"I'm good, thanks." Summer's voice was light and skippy as she trotted off down the hallway. "I am going to Mum's. She's running late. I'm hoping Dad hurries up with food."

"That's all you ever do. Eat, sleep and moan."

Summer glared at her dad before turning the other cheek to ignore him and continue her conversation with Karen.

Zac served up dinner and without waiting for her dad to sit, Summer piled in huge mouthfuls whilst attempting to carry on her conversation with Karen. She ignored Zac's pleas to not talk with food in her mouth. Zac shook his head in resignation as Karen smiled.

The doorbell rang not long after and Summer went to answer it. There were hushed conversations in the hallway before Summer returned, with a woman stomping in behind her.

Summer stood by Karen. "Mum, this is Karen. Karen, this is my mum, Michelle. I'll go get my stuff," Summer added before breezing off upstairs. Her heavy footsteps reverberated through the walls.

Michelle threw a cold frosty stare in Karen's direction and looked her up and down, before rolling her eyes. "Who are you?"

Karen was taken aback by Michelle's clipped tone. Michelle had sharp features, with inflated lips. *Fillers.* Her hair was cut short, bleached blonde and reminded Karen of Annie Lennox in her heyday.

"Michelle, Karen's my partner. We've not been seeing each other for long. I'd like you to be civil towards her…" Zac said firmly.

Michelle glared at him as she came over and rested her hands on the table. "I don't need to be civil to anyone," she hissed.

Karen stiffened and buttoned her mouth, not wishing to inflame the situation. She'd already taken an instant dislike to the woman. Every sinew of her body wanted to get up and knock Michelle across the room.

Zac sniffed the air. "Have you had a drink?"

Michelle tutted before closing her eyes. "I had one measly glass of wine at lunchtime. Okay…?"

"I didn't want you to be over the limit, for your sake and… Summer's."

"Thanks for your *concern*, but I can care for *my* daughter," she hissed through clenched teeth.

"I know," Zac said, holding up his hands to pacify her.

No one said anything for a few minutes. The atmosphere felt tense and prickly. Karen noticed his hands curled into fists.

"I'd like to say it was a pleasure meeting you, Karen, but it wasn't. He'll soon get bored with you. I'm the love of his life. That's why he's finding it so hard to let go."

Zac stepped in and closed the gap with Michelle. His voice was low but firm so Summer wouldn't hear. "I asked… you… to… be… civil. If you can't be, then leave. You have no say in my life now, and our only connection is Summer," he hissed, wagging a finger in her face. "In future you can wait outside for her."

Michelle turned and headed for the door, shouting to Summer that she would be waiting in the car.

Summer dashed out, saying her goodbyes from the hallway before disappearing.

Zac and Karen sat in uncomfortable silence. Karen didn't know what to say, appalled by the woman's behaviour and Zac's response.

Finally, she couldn't contain herself any longer. Zac had hardly made eye contact with her since Michelle had left. "What the fuck just happened there?"

Zac looked up, "I need to tell you something."

56

"Will you please tell me what's going on?" Karen prompted. In the space of a few minutes Zac had changed into someone she hardly recognised. He was silent, his arms tucked into his sides, and for a moment he looked like a boy who'd been scolded by his parents.

"I don't know where to start, so I'm just going to tell you everything. I'm sorry about the way that Michelle talked to you. She likes routine and doesn't like surprises being sprung on her. Hence the frosty reception."

"I can deal with that. But I won't lie, I was surprised."

"Michelle has always had *issues* around my access rights with Summer. She wanted full custody and painted me out as a bad father. She told her solicitors that I used to drink a lot, gamble and have violent outbursts. She also told them that I didn't have a very good relationship with my daughter."

Karen listened. "Was any of that true?"

"No. Absolutely not. Michelle has a very stressful job. It involves highly pressurised meetings, sales pitches, and entertaining clients. As her career took off, she's ended up doing more of the entertaining. A big part of her job is taking clients out to lunches and dinners. It's gone from having one glass of wine socially to several glasses of wine, to her coming home in a cab blind drunk. She is now a heavy drinker."

Karen felt confused. She wasn't sure where this was going but remained silent.

"When we were together, I didn't like it when she came home drunk. Michelle would make so much noise and swear around the house she'd often wake Summer. I never wanted Summer to see her mum like that, so I'd try to calm Michelle down. But she would end up taking it out on me. And as the months and years passed, it got worse."

Karen narrowed her eyes as she studied Zac. The first signs of apprehension prickled her skin as her chest tightened.

"It started with lots of verbals. She was moody, agitated, and awful. And by the next morning when she was sober it was like nothing had happened and she'd turn on the affection."

Karen read between the lines. She'd faced this exact situation countless times. She got out of her chair and stepped around the table, pulling a chair alongside Zac. Karen placed a hand on his lap and examined his crumpled face. He looked broken. "DV?"

Zac took in a deep breath, nodded, and then turned to face her. His eyes were full of tears as he bit his bottom lip. "When I tried to calm her down, she'd lash out at me. Punching, scratching, kicking, take your pick."

Now it made sense to Karen. Every time she'd discussed families or divorce, he'd gone quiet. "Why didn't you say anything?"

"How could I? How can I say, 'oh by the way I'm a victim of domestic violence, nice to meet you!'"

"Wait, did you think I would judge you?"

Zac shook his head.

57

"Why didn't you report this?"

Zac clenched his fists. "I was trying to protect Summer. I didn't want her to find out. I could have dealt with that fallout, but I know Summer wouldn't have. It would have torn the family apart and ruined Michelle's career. She's really proud of her achievements. Michelle hasn't handled the stress very well, that's all."

Karen had seen this many times. The domestic violence victim making excuses for and defending their abuser.

"I understand, but there's support in place to deal with abuse of this nature. Domestic violence goes unnoticed by so many people. How many cases have you been called out to in your career?"

"I hear what you're saying. Look how hard it is for women to find the courage to come forward to report their partners for domestic violence. If they find it hard, can you imagine how hard it is for men?" Zac paused. "How many cases have we dealt with involving a male domestic violence victim? Probably less than half of the cases involve a male victim. Can you imagine how much harder it would be for me, a senior male police officer reporting my wife for domestic violence? Then to have my own force hear about it, and then investigate it…"

Zac sighed and laid his head on the table. Exhaustion gripped his body.

Karen rubbed his back. "Hey, it's okay. I know it's difficult. There are guys up and down the country who've experienced something similar. One in every three DV cases involves a male victim. It does happen. We live in a world where the common idea is of men being tough and macho, but that's changing a little. And as each male victim comes forward, it gives hope for other DV victims, especially men."

Zac looked up at Karen. "You just don't get it. Do you think I feel any better knowing that I'm another victim, another stat?"

"Sorry, I didn't mean that, Zac. I meant…"

Zac slapped his hand on the table, startling Karen. "I couldn't handle the shame! Back then I was a victim. I felt weak and pathetic. I didn't stand up for myself. I kept taking everything Michelle threw at me because I loved her. I didn't want to be that person walking down the corridors and see people whisper behind my back as I passed them. 'There's the fucking coward who couldn't stand up to his missus.' I couldn't have handled that. All we ever hear is women DV victims to the point where it's not taboo to talk about it any more. But men… it's still not talked about out in the open."

"Filing for divorce was your way of getting out of it?"

"Yeah. I wanted to get on with my life. I stuck it out for as long as I could. I wanted to protect Summer, but I couldn't be that person any more. And that didn't go down well either. Her drinking problem and the subject of divorce took the violence to a different level. She stabbed me with a fork once. I was discussing our divorce during dinner and without warning she leant across the table and rammed a fork into the back of my hand." Zac rubbed the back of his right hand as he recalled the moment.

"Getting away from Michelle gave me space to breathe. It stopped the waves of panic that made me shiver. I hated coming home. Having Summer stay with me now keeps me alive. I don't know where I would be without her... Probably at the bottom of the river."

"Please don't say that, Zac." A cold chill raced through Karen as a ghastly vision clouded her thoughts.

"Every time Summer goes up to bed, I sit here and think about how I've let myself down. How I let her down. I'll carry that guilt with me till my last breath on this earth."

"Zac, you didn't let anyone down. You've got nothing to feel guilty about. Michelle controlled you. She manipulated you. You're not at fault."

"It didn't feel that way. If I'm honest, I can barely tolerate the sight of her. I've changed. I've accepted my past. I've dealt with the pain and moved on."

"I'm sorry, Zac. I'm really sorry you had to go through that." Karen reached out and held his hands as her eyes misted and her lip trembled. She felt his pain and agony. She hated the thought that the man she was falling in love with carried such deep and emotional scars. "I'm not here to judge you or your marriage. You've had a profound impact on me. Yeah, you were an annoying sod when I first met you, but you've grown on me."

Zac snorted and sniffed loudly. "I'll take that as a good thing," he replied, as he stared into her eyes, searching for comfort.

"It's definitely a good thing. I won't make any jokes about me wearing the trousers in this relationship then…"

They both laughed before he leant over and captured her soft lips. She could taste his salty tears as he kissed her deeply. Karen wanted him. She needed him. Karen got up from her chair and sat astride Zac, her body aching to be closer. His growing firmness nudged into her. When the kissing didn't satisfy them any longer, he stood and took her by the hand and headed upstairs.

58

Karen's eyes flickered open. For the past few weeks thoughts of waking in Zac's bed had played on her mind. He'd been the perfect gentleman every time they'd spent time together, but a part of her had wanted him to drop the nicey chivalrous thing and let passion take over.

It didn't feel strange as she lay in Zac's bed allowing her eyes to focus and her brain to engage. There was none of the awkwardness of waking up beside a stranger and doing the walk of shame from wherever they'd ended up.

This was different. There was meaning and something Karen had wanted for so long. His warm arms were wrapped around her waist, and his chest hair tickled her back. She smiled to herself. *Is this real? Is this really the start of something good? I hope so.*

Her mind dipped back into the memories of last night. Her skin had tingled in anticipation and excitement as they'd undressed before exploring each other's bodies, savouring every moment of their lovemaking.

"Morning, you ok?" Zac growled, his voice croaking through a dry mouth.

Karen rolled over and faced him. She stared into his eyes. His painful confessions which led to so many tears were a distant memory. He looked calm… and relieved. "I am now," she replied, leaning in to kiss him.

"Are we okay?"

Karen studied Zac through narrowed eyes. "Of course we are. Why do you ask?"

"Because of everything I said last night."

Karen stroked his face. "Everything is fine. I promise. I'm glad you found the courage to tell me. I can't imagine how difficult it was for you to bottle it up, let alone speak up and tell me."

"It does feel better," Zac replied, letting out a long sigh. "I just didn't want you to judge me, and think I wasn't man enough to stand up to her."

"Shsssh, I'm not here to judge anyone. You were in a very difficult situation, and I completely understand. There are thousands of men and women who suffer in silence, scared to speak up or to get help. Whether it's mental, emotional or physical trauma, each one of them struggles to cope with life on a day-to-day basis." Karen wanted to say that everything was going to be okay, but she couldn't erase the memories that haunted him. "I know that you stuck it out because of Summer, and you were putting her feelings first. But everyone reaches a breaking point…"

"Yep."

They cuddled in silence, not wishing to lose the moment.

Zac finally dragged himself away to make coffee. Karen threw on her top and went down to join him, feeling a rush of energy and excitement surge through her body. She carried a skip in her step and a smile that ached her cheeks. They'd hardly finished the coffee before Zac pinned her against the kitchen worktops. The sight of Karen in a blouse that stretched across her naked breasts stirred the animal instinct in him as he took her again. Their bodies quivered as the moment seized them both.

59

Karen felt upbeat this morning as she drove to work. A warm feeling nestled inside her from the night of lovemaking. Her mood had been buoyed further after a text message from her team with the news Spiky had been arrested in the early hours of the morning. Following a call of a disturbance at a local off-licence, officers attending saw the suspect escape from the scene. A short foot chase and a violent scuffle resulted in his capture. One of the officers required hospital treatment after being punched and bitten.

By sheer coincidence it turned out to be Spiky.

"Has he said anything yet?" Karen asked as she stood outside of the interview suites with Belinda.

"Nope. He was violent and aggressive when they brought him in. He's had a few hours in the cells to cool down."

He was every bit the unsavoury character that Karen had imagined. He was dirty and smelly. The only clean thing about him was the white paper suit he was dressed in after his clothes had been removed for forensic analysis. His hair was greasy, long and bedraggled. Karen recognised the scar across his face. A web of tattoos crept up his neck before wrapping around towards his ears. More tattoos stretched across the back of his hands and fingers. His beard was patchy and unkempt. But Karen was really drawn to the man's eyes. They were wide and fixed as if he were staring her out. They twitched occasionally as he ground his teeth.

No wonder he's feared by so many who sleep on the streets.

"Spiky, my uniformed colleagues will be dealing with you about the shoplifting and assault of a police officer. I want to speak to you regarding a different matter," Karen began, glancing down at her file and a picture of a smiling Aleem Noor.

"We've had credible information from an eyewitness that you were involved in an argument and fight with Aleem Noor who was found beaten to death." Karen pulled Aleem's photo from the file and slid it across the table. "Do you recognise the man in this picture?"

Spiky studied the photograph. He remained expressionless. If he recognised Aleem, he showed no sign of it.

Karen continued to push, throwing questions which were met with a wall of silence. Whichever angle she tried proved fruitless. There was nothing there. No reaction. No emotion. Karen needed to draw him out. They'd been interviewing him for fifteen minutes with nothing more than monosyllabic answers and "no comment" at best.

"We believe you've intimidated and attacked other homeless people, robbing them of their personal possessions. Is that correct?"

Belinda seemed equally frustrated with the interview and leant back, her notepad practically empty.

"We believe that you intimidated him and stole his belongings, namely a rucksack which contained his most precious possessions from his native country. When Aleem came looking for you in the hope of retrieving his possessions, you brutally attacked him. Why would you do something to someone who had suffered so much already?"

Spiky glared at Karen. The corner of his lips lifted into a smile.

"Are you that much of a coward that you have to pray on those weaker than you to get your kicks?"

Karen knew she had finally got to him as his eye twitched.

"Does it make you feel more of a man?"

"I don't know who this bloke is. You're wasting your fucking time."

Karen threw him the biggest smug smile she could muster to wind him up. "I disagree. You thought you'd got away with it. Nicking someone else's possessions, only to find that Aleem was prepared to stand up to you and get his stuff back. He made you feel this big…" Karen added, forming a tiny gap between her thumb and index finger.

Spiky slammed his fist on the desk. "No one fucking speaks to me like that, not even you. You fucking talk to me like that again and I'll spread your guts across this table."

"Excellent. We'll add threatening a police officer to your list of charges. Keep them coming. We're just getting started. You're doing a great job of screwing yourself over." Karen laughed as she folded her arms across her chest and dropped her head to one side.

This fuelled Spiky's anger further as he drew in air through his clenched teeth.

"Is this how you felt when Aleem stood up to you? Someone made you look like a right prat? A first-class... prat!"

"I told you I don't know who you're talking about," he spat back, his voice simmering with rage.

Karen lifted the clear evidence bag by her feet and placed it on the table. Inside was Aleem's rucksack. "If you don't know what we're talking about, this is Aleem's rucksack that you had on you when arrested. We've had a look inside and there are pictures of Aleem with his family, religious books, and a few items of clothing. What were you doing with this in your possession?"

Spiky shrugged. "I found it on the floor."

"Convenient. I'll ask you again, did you violently attack Aleem Noor, which subsequently led to his death?"

"Go fuck yourself," Spiky fired back.

Karen smiled. She needed him to stew longer. "I'm suspending the interview here and returning you to your cell whilst we conduct further enquiries. My uniformed colleagues will interview you next."

60

A waiting game followed as Karen returned to her office. Spiky's clothes would be analysed, including the big red Adidas jacket he was seen wearing on the night of Aleem's attack. Initial examination of the clothing identified dark splatter marks which Karen believed to be blood. Scrapings and swabs had been taken to further enhance the forensic investigation.

Spiky would be processed and interviewed by uniformed officers which gave Karen the opportunity to get the findings from forensics.

"Morning," Jade chirped as she trotted into Karen's office.

"Morning, my lovely, and how are you on this bright and breezy day?"

"You do realise it's really cloudy and miserable outside?" Jade replied.

"I do, Jade. But things are looking up. We have our prime

suspect of Aleem's murder in custody and I'm hoping forensics help to nail him."

"Excellent. I'll get up to speed on that right now. But you also look different this morning. I can't quite figure out why. But it looks like you've had a facelift. Everything looks plump and rosy… and well… lifted. It's like you've knocked ten years off your life." Jade leant against the door frame and laughed.

Karen shook her head. "You cheeky mare. Just because I've got a bit of make-up on today and have a spring in my step… I don't know. You can go off people very quickly," Karen said, jabbing a finger in Jade's direction.

Jade eyed her with suspicion. "No, there's something else."

"Well, you're a crap detective if you can't figure it out, so bugger off and do some work," Karen fired back before ushering Jade out of her office, reminding her in the process that they needed to head out and track down Heidi Moreno and Gary Cowan this morning.

Jade was right. She did feel different today but wasn't about to spill the beans. For the first time in ages, she felt more settled in her life. The challenge of a new job filled her with renewed vigour. It was also the prospect of starting life in a new city, and then of course this *thing* with Zac. Karen kept calling it a *thing* and didn't know what else to call it. *Is it the start of a fantastic relationship?* A relationship with the prospect of living under the same roof together? Karen's heart pounded faster. That sounded so grown-up. She'd not found herself in a situation like this. Perhaps that was why a ball of anxiety swirled around inside her stomach.

Karen picked up her phone and reread the sexy text from Zac.

I loved every minute of last night and this morning was just amazing. I can't wait to hold you again. Z xx

Her cheeks ached from smiling. She'd fired off a text seconds later telling Zac she felt the same. Karen sat back at her desk as her mind ran over yesterday evening. It wasn't just the intimacy that meant so much to her. She'd seen a different side to Zac. His vulnerability clear to see when Michelle turned up. She shook her head in disbelief as an image of Zac popped into her mind. His face looked haunted by painful memories. He was right. There was this macho brave image of men.

Domestic violence against women was finally getting more airtime and attention. She'd seen it first-hand. Police were taking more decisive action, conviction rates were increasing, and support services were in place to help the most vulnerable. But that wasn't the case for male victims of DV. She understood the pain he must have suffered especially because of his position. Her heart went out to him.

Karen couldn't change his past, but she was determined to make his present something he looked forward to each morning he opened his eyes.

61

The address for Heidi Moreno took them to an HMO property. Again, it was an area not familiar to Karen. Nether Poppleton was a small sleepy village north-west of the city centre. The contrast couldn't have been more different from where they'd just left. Scenic views, a slower pace of life and quieter streets.

The house they were looking at was a smart semi-detached with a long driveway that skirted along the side of the property towards a garage at the rear. The garden was well maintained in much the same way that all the frontages were along the street. A woman dressed in nothing more than a skimpy sports bra and blue three-quarter length leggings answered the knock on the door. Her dark hair was pulled up high in a ponytail, her strong features giving a hint of her Spanish roots.

"We are looking for Heidi Moreno," Karen asked, holding up her warrant card.

"That's me. Can I help?" she asked.

"May we come in for a few moments? It's about a case we are working on at the moment and thought you might be able to help us with a few questions."

Heidi pursed her lips in confusion but waved them through to the lounge. Two large, three-seater, dark brown leather sofas took up a large proportion of the space, with a dark oak coffee table in the middle of the room. Several cushions sat along the low deep window ledge and offered a perfect vantage point over the street.

"It's a nice place here. Does it cost much?" Karen asked out of interest.

"It's pretty reasonable to be honest. I pay a hundred and five pounds a week including bills, and I have the loft room."

Karen could imagine herself living in a place like this one day... and then a picture of her and Zac cuddled up on the sofa in front of the TV flashed through her mind. *My Lord, what is happening to me?* She brushed aside the thought and returned to the purpose of their visit.

"We are investigating the murder of Beth Hayes and speaking to everyone who came into contact with her to build a better picture of her life."

Heidi wrapped her arms around her chest and nodded. "Yeah, I heard about that through the climbing club. I can't believe it."

Karen exchanged a slight glance with Jade. "We were examining her Facebook profile and identified a couple of people who Beth had blocked. Your name was one of them. We're curious to find out why?"

Heidi rolled her eyes. "Listen, it's no big deal. I didn't really know Beth that well. I knew her through a couple of the climbing groups. When you get to know me, you realise that I'm a bit in-your-face, a bit rude. I can come across as cocky. But that's the Spanish in me. We can be outspoken, a bit fiery, and tend to say what's on our mind rather than keeping it to ourselves."

"Did something happen between you and Beth?"

"Not really. I can be loud. And I'm really passionate about my climbing. Beth and I have been on a couple of group climbs, and when I'm there I'm really fired up. I'm competitive. I like winning, and I like to be out there with the lads."

"And Beth didn't like that?" Karen asked.

"We were different. Don't get me wrong. She was popular. But I'm a bit of a tomboy so can get gobby. I heard from others that Beth found me a bit *abrasive*, so I confronted her about it and told her not to be so uptight." Heidi laughed and shrugged. "I guess she didn't like me being in her face, and the next thing I was blocked. It's no big deal for me. Fuck it. I don't mean any harm. It's the way I am."

"I see. Where were you on Monday morning between seven a.m. and ten a.m.?"

Heidi scowled at Karen. "Am I under suspicion?"

"It's standard for elimination purposes and we're asking every person who came in contact with her."

"I work at Cooper's building products in town. I'm an accounts assistant. I start work at eight o'clock. You can check if you want," Heidi fired back.

"Okay, thanks for your time. I think that will be it. Oh, one last question. Did you ever notice anyone acting suspiciously around her or giving her a bit too much attention?"

"Not that I can think of."

62

En route to Gary Cowan, Jade put in a call to Cooper's building products. They confirmed Heidi as an employee who'd clocked on at eight a.m. every day this week but had the flexibility in her hours to start and finish later.

With her alibi checking out Heidi could be scratched off their list of suspects for the moment. In the back of her mind Karen still wondered if there was a side to Beth that they hadn't yet uncovered. On the face of it she appeared a kind, caring and energetic woman who embraced the outdoors and loved climbing. Beth appeared to get on with everyone and didn't have any enemies.

Adam Taylor was the only one who appeared to have the slightest motive for wanting to harm her. The transcript of their messages showed that he was unhappy and shocked at the pregnancy news, and had even suggested a termination at one point. With Beth carrying his child, the bombshell was enough to wreck his relationship with his girlfriend,

Fiona. But Fiona supported his alibi which meant that Taylor was nowhere near the scene.

"Cowan lives here?" Jade remarked as she stared in disbelief.

The address for Gary Cowan had taken them to a small apartment block. It looked like a 1960s construction in desperate need of repair. Silver aluminium window frames had tarnished in the sunlight. The path leading up to the door was cracked. Weeds crept through and the front door to the block was a sprawl of colourful graffiti. Black bin liners of rubbish spilt over a large wheelie bin.

Karen checked her phone again. "Yep, this is the address we've got." She pressed the buzzer. A few seconds passed before someone answered.

"Hello, it's the police. We have a few questions. Can you let us in?"

An answer didn't come but the door buzzer sounded regardless. The outside was bad, but the inside took filth to a whole new level. The smell of stale urine filled the corridors, discarded rubbish boxes sat outside a few of the doors and mouse droppings dotted the tiled floor.

Karen sighed. *How can people live like this?*

Jade pulled back her lips in horror. "Oh my God. Oh my God! I think I'm going to be sick. Can't I wait outside? I've left my hand gel and gloves in the car. Wait a sec whilst I go and get them."

Karen looked at Jade and laughed. "You're getting worse. You really have a problem with cleanliness and germs, don't you? Did you hear the joke about the germ? Never mind. I don't want to spread it around."

Jade slapped her hands as a shiver ran down her spine. "Stop. Enough!"

"Did you know that mouse and rat droppings give off bacteria dust that if inhaled create large boils on the lining of your lungs?"

Jade's eyes widened in sheer terror as her gaze darted towards the droppings that littered the floor all around her. Her breath was short and sharp as the panic swelled inside her. "Fuck. I'm going to sit in the car before I have a full-blown panic attack. Is that true?"

Tears streamed from Karen's eyes as she shook her head. "No idea. But it made you shit yourself."

Jade slapped a hand over her face before swiftly pulling it away and staring at it as if it was germ infested. "Why? Why would you do that? You're so nasty sometimes."

"Sorry. I couldn't help it." Karen knocked and waited for a few seconds before a dark-skinned man opened the door. The whites of his eyes were like two large white snooker balls as they stared at Karen.

"Yes, what is it?" he asked, his accent thick with an African drawl.

Karen held up a warrant card. "We are looking for Gary Cowan. We have this apartment as his last known address."

The man knew nothing of Gary Cowan and had been renting the apartment for just under a year through the council. He provided Karen with the name of his letting agent. Whilst Jade put in a call to them, Karen knocked on a few other doors. The picture they were building of Cowan concerned Karen. The letting agent had been assigned by the council to offer him reasonable accommodation.

However, according to neighbours he hadn't stayed long and the first the letting agent knew about it was when they visited to find the place unoccupied. They were met with squalid and messy conditions. Many of the neighbours commented on how Cowan never spoke to them and appeared introverted. He rarely came out of his apartment, only venturing out late into the night when no one was around. Cowan had no visitors and they believed he didn't work.

"I've got a rough idea of where he is based on feedback from the neighbours," Karen said as she joined Jade outside. "He is with another letting agent. Can you call them to get an address?" she added, passing the number on to Jade.

63

Gormire Lake held a magnetic attraction that kept pulling him back. He'd already enjoyed a solitary walk and the stillness. The walking trail around it was four miles long and enough for him. It offered the perfect vantage point to marvel at Whitestone Cliff.

He perched on a rock and admired the view. James Herriot once called this view "the best in England" and he could see why. The lake was surrounded by a forest in the valley bottom and was formed by glacial erosion over twenty thousand years ago. There was so much history in this place. Gormire translated as "filthy swamp" and its dark appearance gave rise to several myths including that it was bottomless and concealed the remains of a sunken village.

He had been to this place so many times, agreeing with the reports that the lake and Garbutt Wood had an "otherworldly" and "fairy tale" quality. In his mind it was where dreams would come true… or where dreams would end.

The vast expanse of water stretched out around him as dark and still as his mind. Why had he been so stupid as to think that she would listen to him? He'd been infatuated with her since first clapping eyes on her. Naturally beautiful, exciting, energetic, and sexy. But then every other man who seemed to come within a five-foot radius of her appeared to be mesmerised by her beauty.

Twisting off the cap on his flask, he poured a steaming cup of coffee. Steam swirled and danced. He weighed up the flask in his hand. These little two-cup jobbies made the perfect travelling companion. Easy to slot into the side of his rucksack and not too heavy. He marvelled at their creation. How had he gone for so long without one?

He stared up towards the cliff edge and wondered what it would have been like sitting here watching Beth fall from such a height. His mind tracked back to seeing her nails claw through the loose earth in a desperate and pathetic attempt to save herself. A shiver ran through him. It had sounded like nails being dragged over a blackboard.

But then again… she'd had it coming to her. She'd made him more miserable than happy, and despite how much he'd loved her, he'd needed to let her go. He didn't want anyone else to experience having her.

Why did people love you but hate me? Was it because you were a beautiful lie, and I was a painful truth?

The emptiness of his surroundings sat deep within his stomach. He was neither sad nor angry.

He'd read a quote once, "When there's no more room in hell, the dead will walk the earth."

Is that why I'm still here?

He stood and walked to the edge of the lake and stared down at the black abyss. As black as tar, and as dark as death, he felt at one with it. He held out the bag containing the Karrimor boots and jacket, its pockets weighed down with rocks. After he released his grip, the bag splashed into the water. Its outline disappeared into the inky blackness, never to be seen again.

64

Burgsy's seemed like the best place to stop for lunch as Karen waited for the letting agent to get back to them. She'd heard a few people in the office rave about this American burger bar and decided that they deserved a treat.

From the outside it looked like a traditional old pub with brown window frames and a brick façade. But once inside it smacked of the good ol' US of A from the high bar stools and counters to the wall art of cowboys and their horses out in the wilderness.

Karen and Jade pored over the menu whilst their waiter walked them through the options before taking their orders.

"I'm not going to get through all of this!" Jade said in surprise when their food arrived. The burgers were works of art that stood so tall, Jade wondered how she'd even pick it up let alone get her mouth around it.

It was one of those rare opportunities where they could relax and forget about work. Karen had missed that over the last few weeks. It was something she used to look forward to when they picked a random and obscure restaurant to let off steam and have a catch-up.

"How do you think you're settling in?" Karen asked in between mouthfuls of burger.

"It's been really good. I won't lie. I was quite nervous and worried about making the move. I wouldn't have done it if you weren't here. But I'm glad I have. Everything you said was true."

Karen threw Jade a wry smile. "Did you think I was making it up?"

"No. No." Jade laughed. "The way you described the team, the environment, even the offices, seemed a bit too good to be true. If you know what I mean?"

"I do. I was surprised to say the least when I saw it for myself. We have a really good chance here to make a name for ourselves. The teams are small, the hierarchy flat, and there's less competition. I want us to both do well, and that's why I deliberately didn't appoint a DI. I convinced Laura that I wanted you as my number two. With the right training and responsibility, I know you can do it."

Jade's heart swelled and her eyes misted. "I can't thank you enough, Karen. I really want to do well in my career and becoming a DI would be a dream come true. Of course, I'd be chasing a DCI role after that, so you'd better watch out…"

"Well, that's settled then. I'll do whatever I can to get you there."

"Thanks, Karen. I think Bel is really nice too. She's really helping me to settle in."

"Yep, I agree. Not a bad bone in her body."

"Bel took me on The Bloody Tour of York. It was fascinating to see the darker history of the city. That Mad Alice was born for that role. She was a brilliant host and took time to speak to everyone. She included us in the stories and kept us laughing throughout."

"You've done better than me. Zac said he'd take me and still hasn't," Karen said.

"Talking of Zac, how are things going on that front?" Jade winked.

"Surprisingly well, touch wood." Karen tapped the table. "I'm surprised I've not put him off. We're getting on really well. In fact, I stayed at his last night for the first time."

Jade's eyes widened in surprise. She wagged a finger in Karen's direction. "I knew it. You still had that rosy glow on your face this morning. Do I need to buy a hat?"

"Get off. I've only started seeing him."

They both laughed as they continued with their lunch. It was what they'd needed. The chance to reconnect as friends and chill.

65

Not long after finishing their lunch, the second letting agent came back with a new address for Gary Cowan. The journey took them to Kirkham Abbey, north-east of their location.

Karen pulled over to one side to get her bearings. It was a beautiful location in Karen's opinion, and she imagined that in a few months there would be a constant stream of visitors to the area. Her eyes were drawn to the mediaeval ruins of Kirkham Priory which sat on the bank of the meandering River Derwent. She'd crossed the small river, traversing a beautiful stone bridge with three sweeping arcs that plunged into the still waters. As Karen glanced back over her shoulder, the river was framed like a John Constable painting with a rich green border of trees that met the sky.

"He's certainly picked a good location to live. Quiet. Remote. Hardly a soul around."

Jade marvelled at the rich, green landscape and murmured in agreement.

Karen checked her satnav before moving off and turning left into a small and narrow dirt track that skirted through ten feet tall hedgerows. As she crawled through the track, the hedgerows appeared to creep in on her, making the gap tighter. The track eventually opened out to a dead end and a solitary small cottage.

Karen and Jade stepped from the car and scoped the surrounding area. A deathly silence enveloped them. No wind. No vehicles. No people.

"I wouldn't want to be stuck here on a dark night. I bet you there's no light pollution whatsoever," Karen said, staring up towards the sky.

"I know. Imagine if it snowed. I could be stuck here for weeks. I could die of starvation. What would happen if I fell ill? Would a doctor or ambulance even come all the way out here?"

Karen crossed her arms and raised a brow. "Jade, why do you always think of the worst-case scenario in every situation?"

"I don't. But imagine if it was you."

"Thank God you're not in the States. You'd be one of those preppers."

"What's one of them?" Jade asked.

"Look it up later," Karen replied as she headed off towards the cottage. Karen knocked on the door and waited a few moments before knocking again. Realising no one was home, she moved around towards the nearest window and peered in through the grubby panes of glass. Karen struggled to see clearly. Whilst Karen headed one way, Jade went the other. Karen moved around to the side of the building and checked the bins. Discarded food containers, milk cartons, and local newspapers filled them.

After slapping on a pair of latex gloves, Karen pulled out one of the newspapers to check the date. A copy of the local rag from last week confirmed that someone had been living here. The milk carton showed a use-by date of three days ago. Karen rummaged further in case there was anything else of interest before moving to the rear of the property where she met up with Jade.

"Any joy?" she asked Jade.

"Nope. You?"

Karen told her about the evidence in the bin. "Perhaps he's working or out and about at the moment. We'll try again tomorrow." Karen made a mental note to have officers pay another visit later on this evening in the hope that they would be luckier than her.

66

Having returned to the office later on that afternoon, Karen spent the next few hours checking system updates from her team and going through emails that cluttered up her inbox. *At least one thing never changes*, Karen thought to herself as she ploughed through the usual internal memos, briefing updates, and messages that held no relevance.

Karen checked her watch. It was fast approaching seven p.m. She had a few more bits and pieces to do but needed a break to rest her eyes. Pushing her chair back, she headed for the kitchen to rustle up another cup of coffee. She glanced through the glass partition towards the main SCU floor. Most of her officers had headed home for the evening, with just a few remaining who would cover overnight. It reminded her that she still needed to sit down with each team member to go through their PDP. Each officer's personal development plan was not only crucial for their own development but helped with the force's succession planning. She didn't want to be one of those DCIs who were so wrapped up in their own self-interest that they often ignored the ambitions of the officers in their command.

She was excited for Jade. Karen was confident that Jade had the intellect, personality, and drive to make a name for herself in the force. When the next case came along, Karen wanted to make Jade acting SIO which would give her the opportunity to stretch her wings and challenge herself.

Karen had put in a quick call to Zac earlier. He was already at home with his feet up in front of the sofa having a cuppa. With the thought of him being there alone, Karen wanted to drop everything and dash over to his place. She not only wanted to be there for him after his revelations of the night before, but her body ached for him again. With it being Sunday morning tomorrow, the prospect of having a long, sleepy lie-in with him seemed irresistible. The suggestion was on the tip of her tongue, but she held back. *Is it being too pushy? Will it come across as being needy? Will I be crowding his space?* Karen reached for her phone and began to punch out a message to him.

The sound of clapping from the main SCU floor jolted her from her thoughts and phone. She grabbed her mug and headed back to see what all the noise was about.

"Karen!" someone shouted. "We've got a result on Aleem's case."

Karen dashed over towards the desk of a junior officer, excitement pulsating through her.

The female officer shoved a warm piece of paper that was fresh off the printer in Karen's hand. "We've got the forensic breakthrough. They've identified tiny blood splatters on Spiky's clothing and DNA evidence from his nail scrapings. They are a match to Aleem Noor."

Karen punched the air. "Fucking brilliant. Absolutely bloody brilliant."

"It gets better. A plastic water bottle recovered from inside Aleem's rucksack has a partial fingerprint that matches Spiky's prints. There are also traces of Aleem's blood on the bottle. Forensics believe that those traces of blood were more than likely transferred to the bottle after Aleem's attack. Bearing in mind he was found unresponsive at the scene, and his rucksack was missing…"

"They could have only been transferred after the event once the rucksack had been taken," Karen said, finishing off the officer's sentence. "Get on to CPS and present the evidence. Let's see if we can get a charge and get this wrapped up."

"Karen, I already have. CPS gave us the green light to charge Spiky with murder."

It was Karen's turn to clap. "Well done, team. This is a fantastic result."

The smiles on their faces said it all. Karen had hoped for this much-needed break. With two cases running simultaneously, her team had been tested. More importantly for Karen, the spotlight was firmly upon her. She needed to stamp her mark in the force. Laura had drilled it into her that officers were judged on results not likeability.

She left the team celebrating their win and headed back to her office. With the door closed behind her, a cloak of stillness and calm cocooned Karen. Dropping into her chair, she let out a huge sigh of relief and tipped her head back.

Her mind swirled as thoughts skipped from one thing to another. The charge was only the start. The team needed to focus on building the case file ready for court. There would be endless meetings with their force's brief, and she'd need to prepare for her time in court.

Karen's mind turned to Aleem Noor. That particular case came with its own challenges. Working with and gaining the trust of the homeless community was hard in any part of the country. She'd seen her fair share of crimes against the homeless go unsolved due to the lack of cooperation. But at least she could feel satisfied that Aleem's death hadn't been in vain. She'd secured justice for a man who'd come to the UK seeking sanctuary, a better life and the chance of a new start. A fear of authority had stopped him embracing the support on offer in the UK, and sadly he'd paid the ultimate price.

"I need to get out of here, I'm shattered." Karen sighed, rubbing her eyes. A smile softened her features as an idea popped into her mind. She grabbed her phone and sent Zac a text before logging off and leaving.

"On the spur-of-the-moment decision?" Zac said as he crossed the road to join her.

Karen shrugged. "You could say that. I planned on an early night this evening, and you were already at home, so it seemed like a good chance for us to catch up again?"

Zac agreed as he gave her a warm hug and glanced through the windows of the restaurant. "Turkish, good choice. I'm starving. I was about to heat up leftovers when I got your text message."

Karen had picked the restaurant off Google after reading the reviews about Yakamoz, so it seemed like a good place for them to catch up and have a talk. She hadn't booked, but the restaurant managed to fit them in after a short fifteen-minute wait. It looked like a bookshop from the outside but felt warm and inviting as they were seated. The smell of spices, doughy flatbreads and sizzling chicken from the grill wafted across the tables.

"I'm bloody starving now," Karen said as she glanced through the menu. The waiter took their drinks order before returning a few minutes later and guided them through the specials. Karen glanced around the restaurant as she sipped a drink. A few couples were dotted around, with several large family groups huddled around tables towards the rear. The place had a relaxed vibe with low lighting, Turkish music being pumped through the PA system, and laughter breaking out all around them.

Karen breathed a sigh of relief and soaked up the surrounding energy.

Zac reached out and held her hand across the table. She smiled as she felt the warmth in his fingers as his thumb stroked the back of her hand. Zac opened his mouth as if to say something. Karen held her breath wondering what he might say as she stared into his eyes.

"You want that last bit of pitta?" he asked, nodding towards the plate between them.

Karen rolled her eyes and laughed. "For a minute I thought you were going to be dead romantic. Typical bloke, always thinking of your stomach."

Zac recoiled, feigning shock. "How could you think that? I was just making sure that we got value for money. Especially because you're paying."

"You can be a real tosser sometimes." Karen shoved the plate in his direction.

The ribbing continued between them as they ate. Small plates of food continued to arrive as Karen began to regret ordering so much. A singer piped up from the back of the restaurant. The woman's voice drowned out their conversation each time she hit the high notes. The evening relaxed them both.

"Good food, great company and an intimate environment. What more could I ask for?" Karen shouted above the noise.

Zac raised his glass and toasted that sentiment.

Karen glanced around at the other diners. Laughter, smiles, and animated conversations surrounded them. *This is how life should be. I could get used to this*, Karen thought. So much of their day-to-day existence centred around the unsavoury aspects of life that they missed simple pleasures such as a walk in the park, a cheeky meal in the evening, or a popcorn and movie night. Karen would often be mentally and physically tired at the end of a shift. She'd crave the sanctuary of her apartment and a glass of wine.

York gave her an opportunity to change the imbalances in her life and she was determined to embrace them.

The singer took a break which afforded Karen and Zac the chance to sit back, let the food settle and enjoy the ambiance over a coffee. The stress and tightness in her shoulders eased as the evening wore on. Tiredness crept in as Karen stifled a yawn.

"Keeping you up?"

"Sorry, all this food has killed me. I feel like I'm about to give birth to a baby elephant!"

"I know the feeling. I undid the top button of my jeans ages ago," Zac replied as he patted his swollen belly.

"I'll grab the bill and then we can head back. I need to walk off this food." Karen waved over a waiter and did the thing that every diner seemed to do… pretend they're holding a pen and write an imaginary note in the air.

68

Karen draped her arm in Zac's as they walked back. The road was quaint, narrow, and filled with small boutique shops which added charm and character. She loved everything about the place. Every corner and each new street they crossed revealed something new to see.

They walked in silence for a few minutes enjoying the stillness and crisp night air. The heat from the restaurant soon replaced by a blanket of coolness that tightened their skin and invigorated their tired minds.

Karen squeezed his arm. "I'm really proud of what you did last night."

Zac laughed. "I have had sex before you know."

Karen elbowed him in the ribs. "Ha ha, very funny. I'm being serious. I'm talking about the *other* thing."

Zac fell silent as he looked across at Karen.

"It took a lot of courage to open up and tell me. It couldn't have been easy. Thank you for trusting in me."

Karen wrapped her arms around him and squeezed tight before continuing their walk. "Did you ever think about talking to someone about this? Maybe going to a support group?"

Zac shook his head. "No. I couldn't go through with it. The thought of sitting around in a group and admitting I'm a police officer and a DV victim… no. I don't want all those eyes staring at me. They'd think how can I be a copper and still be a victim?"

"They wouldn't think that at all. Besides, you don't have to tell them that you're in the job. Those groups exist for victims to support each other, to work through the pain, the confusion, and to get clarity. I'm sure most of the guys in those groups feel alone and that no one believes them. I think you could really do some good. With your dual perspective you could really help others get through those difficult times. You're a different person now. You're strong, focused and have a fantastic relationship with Summer. You could show guys that there's hope beyond what they're going through."

"Yes, you're probably right. I look back on those days and feel like the stupid one. Michelle tried to justify her outbursts and attacks by telling me about her troubled childhood. The childhood without love or affection. Without stability or continuity. And I fell for it. I felt sorry for her. I tried my best to please her. I tried to follow her rules." Zac stared up at the night sky. Dark as his thoughts. "But there were rules for everything in our day-to-day lives. What we did, what we ate, how she liked things arranged on a plate. Most of the time I could cope. I put it down to her quirkiness. It was the times when she was drunk, or the next day when she had a hangover that were worse."

Zac's words tugged on Karen's heart. She wanted to tell him everything was going to be okay. That she could take away his pain. She wanted to say so many things but held her tongue. Zac needed to talk for his own sanity.

"The phrase 'a bear with a sore head' was an understatement when Michelle was hung-over. I couldn't touch her, come close to her, or even talk to her. It was like everything I said or did felt like a cheese grater in her mind. She'd stand there with eyes closed, her lips pursed tight, and her hands curled in fists." Zac sighed and shook his head as he recalled painful memories. "I'd make a strong cup of coffee and toast in the hope it would help with her hangover, but I couldn't do anything right when she was in that frame of mind. Nothing I did pleased her. 'Bam!' She would punch me in the arm or slap me around the head."

"I'm so sorry. To be honest saying sorry sounds inadequate. I can't begin to imagine how it felt."

"I know, Karen. You don't have to say anything. Other than Michelle and Summer, you are the only other living person who knows about this."

Karen stopped by their cars and turned to face him. She grabbed him by the collar of his jacket and stared into his eyes. "You did not make any mistakes. Do you hear me? Men always find it hard to see themselves as victims of DV. None of this is your fault. Men can often feel powerless in this situation."

"I know that now. At the time it didn't feel that way. Anyway, as I've said, it's behind me now. I'm not that person any more. I let Michelle get into my mind and overwhelm me with her toxicity. Ultimately, I hung on in there for the sake of keeping the family together and for Summer. It was an intolerable situation," Zac replied. "But here we are. Both my daughter and I are stronger and more resilient for it."

"I remember a case in London where a male domestic violence victim plucked up the courage to walk into our station. I interviewed him and documented a long history of DV. He reported that on one occasion his wife stood in front of him, took off her dressing gown and stood there naked. She then proceeded to beat herself, scratch herself and shout, 'Stop it! Please! That hurts!' When she'd finished assaulting herself, she put the dressing gown on again and pulled out her mobile phone which had recorded everything she'd just done. She threatened to blackmail him with the audio if he told anybody about her violence."

"Shit!"

"Exactly," Karen replied. "Listen, you've moved on. Michelle's a nasty piece of work. I really think you could do some good by maybe volunteering at one of these DV support groups? At least think about it, hey?"

Zac leant in and held on to Karen. With their bodies pressed tight against the cold, Zac welcomed the heat and Karen's support. "Okay."

69

The good news continued as Karen woke on Sunday morning. Not only had Spiky been charged with murder but also charged with a common assault offence under the Assaults on Emergency Workers (Offences) Act 2018, a recent law brought in to protect emergency workers after rising attacks and assaults on ambulance staff and police officers.

If the case went her way and Spiky was charged and sentenced for murder as well as the common assault offence, he would be spending the next ten to fifteen years in one of Her Majesty's finest establishments.

Karen pottered around her apartment clearing the clutter but ended up moving it from one end of the lounge to the other. Manky padded around her ankles and followed her from one room to another meowing for attention. Karen wasn't due in for another hour so scooped him up and gave him a much deserved cuddle before heading off to pick up Jade.

Karen updated Jade on their journey back to Kirkham Abbey. Jade sounded disappointed at not being in the office when the results had come in but was pleased. This was what Karen wanted — an opportunity for them to stamp their mark and get noticed by senior management. With the SCU being a new unit, results spoke louder than words. In order for the team to be continually funded in the future, Karen had to make sure that they got results like this quickly.

The journey was as lovely as they remembered yesterday. Jade spotted ramblers criss-crossing the fields, roads and public footpaths as they scanned their Ordnance Survey maps. It was the perfect landscape to explore providing a rich green canvas of rolling hills and woods that formed the southern tip of the Howardian Hills.

Having come to a stop outside of the cottage, Karen and Jade left the vehicle. Uniformed officers had attended Cowan's cottage last night at eleven p.m. and confirmed his absence, so Karen didn't hold out much hope for their second visit.

It gave Karen another opportunity to check the area. The property was certainly off the grid and hard to find as Peter had mentioned. Cowan was either a social recluse or someone who didn't want to draw any attention to himself. Karen realised that people were like that for many reasons. Some searched for a solitary life away from the influences of modern society, whilst others were affected by mental, emotional, or psychological problems and hid themselves away.

Karen hammered on the door again before moving over to the window to look for any signs of movement. Jade joined

Karen as they circled the property tapping on all the windows in case someone was asleep.

"Looks like another wasted journey," Karen said.

"Maybe he is away for a few days?"

Karen shrugged, placing her hands on her hips. "Your guess is as good as mine. But that car wasn't there yesterday," Karen added, pointing towards a small Mini parked about twenty yards away. It was obscured behind trees that skirted the rear of the property and formed the fringe of the forest that crept up a hillside. Karen realised that it was a clever place to hide a vehicle. She'd only spotted it by chance. Casual walkers would probably not even see it or, at the very least, only catch a fleeting glance of it.

As Karen and Jade examined the car, its recent use soon became clear. The bonnet was slightly warm with no evidence of a layer of dust to suggest it being parked up for days, weeks or even months elsewhere.

"Karen, look at this," Jade said as she peered through the side window on to the back seat.

Karen took a quick look and saw a length of rope, a small axe, and a knife.

"Jade, let's head back up the track. We can watch the cottage from a distance. Perhaps from over there…" Karen tipped her head towards a crop of trees that sat in an elevated position overlooking the cottage.

"Do you think Cowan is inside but choosing not to answer?"

"We're about to find out," Karen whispered. "We need to

act normal and move away from the scene in case we are being watched. In the meantime, can you call for backup, just in case."

70

Karen circumnavigated the surrounding fields and popped up in a copse of trees that gave her a clear line of sight to the property. With another unit of officers parked a few minutes away, Karen and Jade waited. Thankfully the air was dry, there was no forecast of rain, and the odd glimmer of blue sky poked through the clouds.

"What happens if we don't see anything over the next hour or two?" Jade asked. "I mean, I might need a pee by then."

Karen laughed. "There are plenty of trees to hide your modesty. You can squat down and do your business."

"Ew! We don't live in the dark ages. I can think of nothing worse."

"Stop thinking about it. The more you do, the more you'll want to go for a wee. Concentrate on the cottage. I don't know, it's like taking a ten-year-old out for the day."

They hovered around in the shadows for the next forty-five

minutes taking it in turns to keep tabs on the property whilst the other walked around to ease the stiffness in their limbs.

Karen's eyes narrowed as she focused in on an upstairs window. She could have sworn there was movement. Was it the clouds drifting across the sky that had cast reflections in the window?

"Jade, come here a sec. Check out the top right window. I can't be certain, but I thought I saw movement."

Jade came alongside Karen and observed for a few seconds before shaking her head. "Nope. I can't see anything."

A few minutes passed before Karen elbowed Jade again. "There... See that?"

Jade agreed this time. From their position a silhouette moved close to the window. Karen radioed through to the other officers to tell them to meet her there.

With Karen and Jade at the front door, uniformed officers circled around to the rear of the property to keep an eye on the back door. Karen hammered on the door with her fist. "Hello. This is the police. Can you open up?" she shouted.

Just as Karen was about to repeat herself, a volley of shouting followed by a scream broke the silence. It came from the rear of the property. Karen and Jade raced to the back. Karen's heart hammered against her chest as her body stiffened. A shot of adrenaline surged through her system. Karen whipped out her baton as she turned the corner.

The female officer lay on the ground curled in a foetal position clutching her stomach as blood seeped through her fingers. Her male colleague had both hands pressed against the wound, attempting to staunch the blood loss. "He came out of nowhere, boss. The back door just flung open, and he raced at us. Angie was the closest to him and as she tried to block his path, he stabbed her."

Angie writhed on the ground, her painful moans and screaming tearing through Karen. The risk assessment jumped from low to high priority in a matter of seconds as Jade called for an ambulance and reinforcements.

"Where's Cowan?"

The male officer pointed a bloodied hand towards the trees.

Karen knew by the time extra officers arrived, and even with the help of NPAS, Cowan would be long gone. The area was remote, with very few roads, and even fewer people. It would be like searching for a needle in a haystack. She had no choice but to go after him.

71

Karen followed a path of trodden grass along a small incline that cut through a dense group of trees before the ground levelled off. Smaller trees reached skyward, doing little to hide an overgrown field beyond. In the middle of it was a small brick shed, possibly once used as a stable for ponies.

Karen scanned the structure. Now dilapidated and rundown, sheets of rusted corrugated iron formed a haphazard roof. A small plastic table and chair sat in front of it with empty soft drink cans. To the right of it was a small fire pit that gave off subtle wooded smoke.

As Karen got closer, she saw the door to the shed was held on with old rusty hinges nailed on to an ageing cracked wooden frame. It certainly wasn't habitable, but if someone wanted to live off the grid, then this was the perfect place for it. Karen stopped. Her eyes darted left to right as her ears tuned in to the surrounding sounds. She heard something. Perhaps it was a rat or fox scurrying around in the overgrown grass. Then she heard it again. At first she couldn't make it out with the grass acting as a soundproofing blanket. Creaking, followed by footsteps. It was coming from behind the shed.

Karen ran around to the side of the building, baton drawn.

In the split second that she turned the corner, Karen didn't have time to react as a lump of wood crashed into her chest, knocking the wind out of her. She staggered back as she held her arms up to protect herself in case of a second blow. Pain thundered through her as she stumbled. Karen gasped for air as she looked up to see Cowan disappear into the next treeline.

"You're not fucking getting away!" Karen shouted as she straightened up.

Cowan made no attempt to hide his escape as he charged through the trees. He left behind a trail of broken branches, kicked up soil, and torn bushes. Though he was out of sight, Karen followed the sounds. She stopped every few minutes to make sure she was heading in the right direction before continuing her pursuit.

Karen was doing everything wrong according to the police rule book. She was going after the suspect unarmed and without backup. But with one officer down already, she had to make a split decision. Jade followed and barked into her radio, but she lagged a few minutes behind. Karen paused for a second realising her vulnerability. Cowan knew this area much better than Karen which did little to boost her confidence. He probably knew a network of footpaths that snaked through the landscape, ones that would hide his escape route. Karen slowed and wondered where some of the paths led when she saw three heading in different directions.

"Fuck."

Further sounds ahead of her gave a clear sign of his location. She raced off again, barking into her radio with an update.

Karen saw Cowan's outline as she closed the gap. Exposed tree roots and bushes made the chase challenging. Cowan tripped and rolled, before getting to his feet and staggering off. His mishap gave Karen the opportunity to close the gap to within a few feet.

"Cowan, stop now. Police! Stop!"

He limped away, giving Karen the opportunity to strike him with her baton. Cowan crumbled to the ground for a moment before rising to his feet. Karen leapt upon him and struck again. Cowan screamed as he tried to scramble away on his hands and knees.

Karen lashed out once more. "Stop fucking resisting!"

Cowan finally collapsed in a heap as Karen sat upon him and handcuffed him. She flipped him over on to his back. He lay there, staring up at the sky, letting out a series of wet gasps. His gaze turned towards her. His stare was piercing and cold. To Karen, it was like staring into the very eyes of evil. They were cold and fuelled with anger. A tear squeezed from the corner of his eye.

"Karen, are you hurt?" Jade shouted, dropping to her knees.

Karen lay a few feet away from Cowan with arms and legs spreadeagled, her eyes skyward as her lungs gasped for breath.

"I'm getting too old for this shit!" Karen groaned as she clutched her chest and rolled over on to her hands and knees. As the adrenaline subsided, pain spread across her body as if she'd run into a wall at ninety miles an hour. From somewhere in the distance came the sound of chopping helicopter blades and sirens. "Where was the cavalry when we needed them?"

"It's not London any more. We're in the bloody sticks. Miles from nowhere. I think we pulled in half of the North Yorkshire police force…" Jade replied, helping Karen back to her feet.

Cowan remained motionless as he was moved into a seating position.

"Gary Cowan, I'm arresting you for assaulting a police officer," Karen began, before reading him his rights and marching him back to the property.

It was a slow and painful trek for Karen. She trailed behind Jade who frogmarched Cowan. His steps were steady, his face sullen, and in marked contrast to how he'd been whilst she'd pursued him.

By the time Jade and Karen returned to Cowan's cottage, they were met with a swarm of police activity. Police cars and 4x4s parked nose to tail down the track. A yellow air ambulance set down close by and a large huddle grew around the rear of the property.

Jade handed Cowan over to another officer who placed him in the rear of the squad car, whilst Karen leant against the side of her car rubbing her chest. Another paramedic checked Karen over and despite their insistence on a hospital check-up, Karen brushed away the suggestion as she demanded to stay until the situation was under control.

Karen saw Belinda and Tyler walking away from the cottage. "What's Angie's condition?"

"They think she's stable. A stab wound to her abdomen. The knife penetrated beneath her stab vest. Unlucky for her, but thankfully the paramedics have stabilised her. They called in the air ambulance because it was quicker. They're about to whisk her off."

Karen felt relieved. No officer could ever prepare for that particular job hazard. She'd been on the receiving end of many routine calls that had turned nasty in an instant. Routine stops on vehicles where the driver had suddenly turned on the officers brandishing screwdrivers or machetes, or turning up at domestics to find the husband, boyfriend or partner attacking officers as they resisted arrest. She'd seen it all in her career, a level of violence members of the public rarely witnessed in their lifetime.

"How are you feeling?" Bel asked as she offered Karen a bottle of water.

"Like I've being hit in the chest with a sledgehammer. Disadvantage of having big boobs. It hurts like hell when you hit them!" Karen mustered a small smile but winced when she laughed. "Fuck. That hurts."

"Maybe you should go to the hospital to be sure? Or go home for a bit? Jade can be acting SIO?"

Belinda had a point and it made sense. There were too many unanswered questions, and she wouldn't rest until she had the answers.

"Maybe I will later, but I want to know why Cowan decided to do a runner."

73

The old brick-built cottage nested in a sea of grass as if conjuring up a happy dream. It had stood the test of time through hail, wind, snow, rain and sun. It provided the perfect sanctuary to be at one with the natural landscape. The inside painted a different picture.

It was hard to tell whether it was a rental property fit for holidaymakers or long-term renters. As Karen walked around the rooms, she noticed the lack of personalisation. They were sparse and provided minimum comfort.

"It's hardly the Ritz, is it?" Jade asked as she trailed behind Karen, poking her head into each doorway she passed.

The ground floor was laid out in a small two-room configuration. A lounge and diner served as one, with a small kitchen to the rear. Various other doors lead to small cupboards and a pantry. A distinctive chill filled the air. Despite the thick stone walls, the flagstone floors offered little warmth. Each footstep echoed around the property.

Karen climbed the steep stairs. The rough white walls

closed in, and the overhead space was tight. *It must have been for dwarfs with small feet*, Karen thought as she made her way up.

There were just two bedrooms up there, a bathroom separating them. The second smaller bedroom with two single beds remained unused with a cot in the far corner. The main bedroom appeared to be the one used by Cowan. The bed was unmade, the duvet hanging off the end. An open suitcase lay on the floor to one side, and a small toiletries bag sat on the dressing table.

Karen snapped on a pair of latex gloves and unzipped the toiletries bag. It contained a few essentials. Spare toothpaste, deodorant, and disposable razors.

Whilst Karen went through the dressing table drawers, Jade checked the wardrobe. T-shirts and jeans hung from a few hangers, and a couple of jumpers were stuffed on the top shelf. "He travels light."

Karen noticed and agreed. The cottage felt sparse with no personal possessions. Karen was a renter too and had framed photographs of her family, friends and holiday snaps dotted around her apartment. She'd personalised her space with rugs, cushions, vases, and ornaments. Everything to make the place feel homely. But she couldn't find any evidence of that here.

"Too light for my liking. I have more stuff than this for an overnight stay in a hotel. Perhaps he has a load of stuff in storage? We'll have to check."

Karen navigated the ridiculous stairs that almost had her toppling forward. She clung to the walls and steadied herself on each step. "This is ridiculous. Who has feet this small?"

"Maybe you have clowns' feet..." Jade laughed from behind.

"Oi, I'm not that big... Am I?"

"You'd make a great Coco the Clown!"

"Oh, shut up you cheeky mare."

Once outside, Karen organised a team of officers to carry out a more thorough search of the cottage. The Mini close to the property had been cordoned off in case it was relevant to her investigation. With more officers arriving at the scene, the place was in danger of being swamped and vital evidence being destroyed.

"What do you want to do with Cowan?" Jade asked.

"Get him off to the nick. We've got enough at the moment to hold him for the attack on Angie. That gives us enough time to go over the place with a fine-tooth comb. I want him in a white paper suit the minute he gets booked in and his clothes bagged up."

"I'll get that sorted. Shall I organise a low-loader to impound his vehicle?"

"If you could Jade, that would be good. I think we need to hang around until the search is completed on the cottage, and forensics has everything they need from where Angie was attacked. There's something not sitting right with me about this place."

74

Karen sat in her car and waited for the painkillers to kick in. Every movement pushed out a gasp for breath. At first, she thought it was broken ribs, though the paramedics on scene suspected that it was bruising more than anything else but still advised her to get properly checked out at the hospital.

Whilst Karen rested, Jade coordinated the troops to make sure the search teams checked the house from top to bottom. Cowan's possessions were documented in readiness for the exhibits officer. It was a few hours before SOCO had given the all-clear for the Mini to be transported back to a holding compound so that it could be pulled apart and examined.

"Angie's undergone surgery. Thankfully, the penetrative wound didn't hit any major organs," Jade said as she returned to the car.

Karen tipped her head back. "That's a relief. I'll try to pop in and see her tomorrow to make sure she's all right," she said as she swung her legs around and pulled herself out of the car. "Fuck, that hurts." She winced through gritted teeth.

"Just sit in the car for a moment, Karen."

"Jade, I've been sat here for over an hour, and everything's stiffened up. If I don't move, I won't be able to get out of the car at all." Karen rocked her shoulders from side to side and felt the jarring pain in her chest like she was being jabbed with a thousand needles.

"Ma'am," an officer shouted as he jogged towards her. "You need to come and see this."

Karen gingerly stepped forward, knowing that each sudden movement could leave her on her knees. She followed the officer through to the kitchen and stared at the floor. A large mat once placed in the middle of the flagstones had been moved to one side. A small wooden door fitted into the floor had been left open for her to examine.

"The search team found this. It's a basement of sorts. You need to take a look."

"Have we got a body?" Karen asked, to which the officer shook his head.

There wasn't going to be any graceful way of descending the steps, so Karen dropped to her hands and knees and crawled to the edge before swinging her legs into the darkened space to find the first step. She took one step at a time before reaching the last rung. She glanced around. Two other officers were already down there as Jade followed her. Karen stepped on to the concrete floor and examined the dark, musty space. It was dimly lit, and from what Karen could make out contained lots of storage boxes, garden furniture that had been packed away for the winter, a few oil heaters, and other household items.

One of the officers beckoned her over to some plastic crates they were examining. Inside were bits and pieces of climbing equipment, as if whoever they belonged to had been making a collection. There were small lengths of climbing rope, carabiners, climbing shoes and gloves. They looked as if they hadn't been used in a while. It was the other plastic crate that drew her attention.

"Jade, have a look at this," Karen said.

"Beth's?" Jade asked as she shone a torch on the discovery.

75

Inside the crate was a black North Face padded jacket and a pink rucksack. Karen unzipped the main compartment to find a pair of socks, a scarf, a thin climbing top and a bottle of water. It was only when she unzipped the front pocket that they had the confirmation they were looking for. A bank card belonging to Beth Hayes.

"Looks like it. We can get forensics to confirm that this was Beth's jacket, and also look for any hair or fibre particles on the coat and rucksack that tie up with Cowan."

On the wall behind the crates hung a large dust sheet. Karen nodded to the officers to take it down. The officers positioned themselves on either side and pulled out the nails that held the sheet in place. As it dropped to the floor Karen stared in surprise and took a step back.

Jade shone her torch on a large plywood board that revealed loads of magazine and press clippings. Dozens of photographs were also pinned to the board. Karen stepped in closer to examine the items. They were all articles about Beth Hayes. A few clippings referred to competitions she'd taken part in whilst others referred to ones she'd won. Karen recognised printouts taken from Facebook pictures. The photographs disturbed her the most — pictures of Beth taken from a distance. Karen assumed with a long telephoto lens. She picked out a few which showed Beth ascending the very same cliff where she'd lost her life. The date stamp confirmed they'd been taken on different days.

Jade tapped the board. "Look at this."

Karen moved alongside her and examined a small collection of photographs tightly packed together. Again, they were taken from a distance but showed Beth and Adam Taylor naked together in the very same spot Karen had followed Taylor to just a few days earlier.

"I can't believe they were being watched," Jade said.

"If they were being watched from a distance, or from somewhere within the trees, it would have been very hard for them to spot anything."

"Ma'am."

Karen turned as one of the officers handed over what appeared to be a notebook pulled out from one of the plastic crates. Karen flicked through the first few pages and read through what appeared to be a journal set out by date and time. A thought crossed her mind. She went back to the small cluster of photographs and checked their timestamps against the journal entries.

Karen read out one corresponding entry. "I watched her fuck him like a whore. Everything inside me wanted to race over and run an axe across the back of his neck. It should be me making love to Beth, not him. Why does she want him and not me? What does he have that I don't?"

Karen picked another timestamp from the photographs and flicked through a few pages until she found the next corresponding entry. "Her nipples were so pointed today. It was cold. Really cold. I could see them perfectly as she sat on top of him. I was desperate to run over and have them to myself. Beth looked beautiful as she tossed her head back. Why is she torturing me like this?"

Each entry Karen checked had a corresponding photograph, even the ones of her climbing.

"How creepy is that…?" Jade said as she sucked in air through her teeth. "He was infatuated with her, or obsessed, or plain deluded."

"We can't be certain that Cowan wrote these. We can get him to give us a handwriting sample for comparison purposes, and if necessary, get a handwriting expert to compare the samples for greater accuracy. In the meantime, we can fast-track forensics overnight."

"I'll arrange for SOCO to get these items bagged up properly," Jade replied as she grabbed her radio.

76

News of the attack on Angie sent shock waves through the team and the station. Every officer understood the dangers of their job, and each one wanted to get home safely to their families every night.

Cowan's arrival was prickly to say the least. Officers glared at him as he was frogmarched across the station car park to the custody suite. The custody sergeant was firm and fair, but behind the smiles bristled a melting pot of anger that one of their own had been attacked by this reprobate.

Since Cowan was kept in the cells whilst the search progressed, it was a few hours before he was taken to an interview room with a live video feed so officers from Karen's team could watch back in the SCU.

Karen and Belinda took a seat opposite Cowan. Karen had chosen Belinda because of her local knowledge which may come in handy whilst they questioned his movements. Cowan accepted the offer of a duty solicitor, who sat beside him. A small Chinese woman, with a pale complexion and blemish-free skin. She kept firing glances in Karen and Belinda's direction from over the top of her glasses.

With the cautions out of the way, Karen took a moment to run through her notes again whilst occasionally glancing across the table. Cowan was younger than she had anticipated. It explained why he had been so quick on his feet. He was twenty-five years old, but barely looked out of his teens. The forensic suit hung from his shoulders and looked two sizes too big for him. He was certainly skinny. Karen's mum would have said that he was the boy down the street who needed fattening up with good home cooking.

His eyes were set deep within dark circles, and his ears stuck out a little. With his copper-coloured hair and freckled cheeks, Karen imagined that he had borne the brunt of schoolboy bullies. He cut a lonely figure as he sat with his arms folded across his chest.

He glared at Karen, not taking his eyes off her. There was nothing there in Karen's opinion. His eyes were soulless, empty... and dead. She was still struggling to get her head around how someone with such boyish young looks could have callously stared at Beth Hayes and cut her rope before watching her fall to her death. *What goes through the mind of such twisted people?* It was a question she had asked herself many times. Each time she sat in front of a killer her burning desire was to crawl inside their minds to figure out how they ticked.

"Gary Cowan, you understand why you've been arrested?"

Cowan nodded and replied for the benefit of the recorder.

"In the course of conducting routine enquiries into the death of Beth Hayes, not only did you do a runner, but you attacked an officer that left her requiring hospital treatment. Why did you run?"

Cowan glanced across to his solicitor who shook her head.

"No comment."

"How well did you know Beth Hayes?"

Cowan shrugged. "Not much."

"Not much? So how do you explain the discoveries in the basement of your home? You appear to show an unnatural interest in Beth's life."

"No I didn't. I just followed her competitions because I knew she was a good climber."

"You climb yourself?" Karen asked.

"A little. But I haven't done for a while. Some of the climbs around here aren't challenging enough."

Karen nodded and smiled. *Bullshitter.* "We have information to suggest that you tried a class to learn how to climb, but encountered... difficulties?"

Cowan scowled in Karen's direction. He wanted to reach across and wipe the smile from her face.

Karen noticed straightaway. Picking through her notes, Karen looked Cowan square in the face. "You see our eyewitness tells us that you failed in a big way. You couldn't get the hang of it and froze. According to their statement you had a panic attack. That doesn't sound like someone who was good at climbing…"

Cowan's jaw stiffened. "They're lying."

"Your phone is now being examined for evidence in

connection with Beth's murder. Is there anything that we may find on there that links you to her death?"

"No. I don't know why you keep asking me about Beth."

"So we won't find any pictures of Beth on your phone? We won't find GPS and cell site data placing your phone either close to where Beth lived, or where she was killed?"

Cowan fell silent and stared at the paper suit, fiddling with a loose thread.

"Let me ask you again. What was your interest in Beth Hayes?" Karen asked, sliding the photographs recovered from the scene across the table in Cowan's direction.

Cowan stared at the naked photographs of Beth astride Adam Taylor. His chin trembled before clearing his throat to compose himself again.

"These were found pinned to the board in your basement. Why would you be taking photographs of Beth having sex with another man in the woods? That feels a little perverted to me... What about you?" Karen asked, turning towards Belinda.

"That's definitely outright pervy on the pervy scale!" Belinda replied with a grimace. "It makes me think that you're a peeping Tom with an unnatural and unhealthy obsession that got off on watching Beth in secret," Belinda replied.

"Would you agree with that?" Karen continued.

"I'm not a peeping Tom."

"You're right. You're not a peeping Tom. The peeping Toms I've come across have pictures of lots of women. *You* only have pictures of Beth. Beth had a creepy feeling she was being followed or watched. Beth was right to think that, wasn't she? It was you."

Cowan shrank back in his chair and glanced at the walls as if they were closing in on him. He nervously bit his bottom lip. "You've got this all wrong."

"Have we? Well, why don't you put us right then? How did we get this so horribly wrong? I mean, what on earth would have possessed us to think that you were carrying an unhealthy obsession towards Beth Hayes?" Karen jabbed a finger at the photographs.

"Okay, I admit that those press clippings were from me. I loved watching her climb. I've been to a few of the competitions. But these photographs have nothing to do with me. Someone must have put them there."

"You're suggesting that you didn't take these photographs, nor did you know anything about them?"

"Correct. I've not been down in that basement for weeks. And I'm out most days doing bits and pieces or just walking, I go down to Gormire Lake to chill. Anyone could have broken in and planted those things there."

Karen nodded and looked down at her notes. She wanted to slow down the interview and buy herself time. "That's possible. But I doubt it." Karen bent down and picked up a clear evidence bag before placing it on the table between them. "Have you seen this before?"

Cowan stared at the exhibit before a brief look of concern stiffened his features.

"I'd like some time alone with my client, detective," the solicitor interrupted.

Karen rolled her eyes. "It works for me. Be my guest. It looks like he needs to wipe the sweat from his brow. Interview terminated."

Cowan and his solicitor were ushered into a separate room to have a confidential discussion away from the cameras.

77

"Bart," Karen said as she breezed into the forensics unit and made her way to Bart Lynch's office.

As the crime scene manager, Bart had been overseeing the evidence recovery process at the murder scene as well as liaising with the exhibits officer each time Karen's team had recovered items of interest.

Bart held up his hand to stop Karen in her tracks. "I know what you're going to say, but I haven't had the results yet."

Karen gritted her teeth. "Bollocks. I really need that information now. That's the whole reason we fast-tracked overnight, and why I have been dragging out the interview."

Bart stood up and came around to join Karen. "I know. It's out of my hands. It's a small fortune to get results prioritised. I was promised them an hour ago. I swear I've been chasing for you."

Karen let out a sigh and leant against the wall. "It's not your fault, Bart. I'm impatient. Cowan's brief is having a word with him at the moment and frankly the longer they talk the better for us. Did you zip over Cowan's prints?"

"Yep. They've got those too. I've asked them to do a comparative analysis along with the other things that you requested. Get yourself a coffee and I'll call you as soon as I hear anything."

Frustration left her edgy as Karen darted off to the SCU. Nervous energy pulsated through her. She needed more information to give her a rock-solid case to throw at Cowan. Her gut instinct told her that he was their man. She now needed the evidence to prove it.

"Jade, how are you getting on with downloading Cowan's phone logs and speaking to his mobile phone provider?"

With the advent of new technology, a few officers including Jade had been trained in the use of specialist software to download phone records from a suspect's phone. This not only reduced the burden on the digital forensics unit but sped up the evidence gathering process.

"I'm pretty much there to be honest. I've compared the timestamps on the photographs with his cell phone records. According to cell mast data, his phone was off on each of those occasions the photographs were taken. And the interesting thing is that his phone was switched off approximately ten minutes before each of those timestamps which suggests that he didn't want to be discovered if his phone rang."

"Bloody brilliant," Karen said, tapping Jade on the shoulder.

"It gets better. GPS coordinates from his phone picked up Cowan's location as being right outside Beth's home address on three separate occasions. And finally, we've also got triangulation data to confirm that he was within five hundred yards of Whitestone Cliff on eleven separate occasions. I would say for at least eighty per cent of the time his phone was picked up in the vicinity of his cottage, or on the outskirts of town, but never in the city centre."

"Never?"

"Nope. There's nothing in the records to suggest he was in town in the last twelve months."

Karen's phone rang. She checked the caller ID and felt her heart quicken. "Speak to me, Bart, but it better be good news?" Karen listened intently, her eyes growing wider as the conversation continued. "Brilliant, you're an angel."

Karen dashed off, grabbing Belinda along the way.

78

Cowan and his solicitor sat patiently in the interview suite waiting for Karen's return. As Karen stepped through the door, the solicitor greeted her with an icy-cold stare.

"My client and I don't appreciate being kept waiting."

"Oh, that's a shame. I'm here to make sure I find the person who killed Beth Hayes, so I'll take as long as I need." Karen slapped a file on the desk and pulled out a chair, with Belinda doing the same beside her.

"Gary, I'll ask you again. What was your interest in Beth Hayes?"

"There wasn't, other than what I've already told you. Listen, I have nothing further to add. My solicitor has advised me everything you've presented so far is circumstantial and you don't have any direct evidence linking me to her death."

"You see, that's where I think you're wrong, Gary. As I said earlier, we've been examining your phone in *detail*. And we've uncovered rather interesting information."

Cowan's eyes narrowed, and his body stiffened as he nervously licked his lips and stared across at his solicitor.

"We have evidence to confirm on several occasions that your phone was near to the cliff where Beth died. Which may tie in with Beth's concerns of being followed."

Cowan shook his head in an arrogant act of disbelief.

"Oh, don't worry, it gets better. We compared the time-stamps on the photographs against your phone. Your phone was switched off ten minutes before each of those photographs was taken. I suggest you switched off your phone to stay undiscovered whilst you spied on Beth and her partner?"

Before Cowan could open his mouth, Karen pressed on.

"GPS data confirms you were less than five yards away from Beth's front door on three separate occasions. What reason would you have to be at Beth's house?"

"Someone must have had my phone," Cowan fired back.

Karen raised a brow. "Convenient. But I don't believe any of that. Shall I tell you why?"

Cowan sat silent; his hands buried deep in his lap.

Karen slid the earlier evidence bag containing a knife across the table. "This knife was recovered from your vehicle. Forensic analysis has confirmed your DNA on the handle and blade, and microscopic polyamide fibres found on the blade edge carried the same structural composition as the rope Beth used. Without doubt we can confirm the blade was used to cut Beth's rope and with no other evidential DNA on the weapon, it also confirms you were in possession of the weapon at the time."

Cowan drew large lungfuls of air in through gritted teeth as he tapped his toes. "You don't know. You don't know anything."

"Gary Cowan, I haven't finished yet. A notebook found in one of the plastic crates in your basement has your prints all over it, which confirms you wrote those journal entries, and each entry is linked to a photograph which places you there when Beth met her partner."

"He wasn't her fucking partner!" Cowan hissed before slamming his hands on the table. "He was with someone else. She rejected me even though I loved her. I loved her from the very first moment I saw her. But she wanted him. It should have been me in the woods. Not Taylor."

"What size shoe do you wear, Gary?"

Cowan smiled. "Eight."

"Is that why you broke into Adam Taylor's car? You stole his things and wore his boots to pin it on him?"

Cowan nodded.

"Can you say that for the benefit of the tape," Karen prompted.

"Yes. I broke into Taylor's car and nicked his stuff. I wanted to get Taylor out of the way. But that didn't stop them from seeing each other. Beth should have been mine. She was beautiful, but she didn't want me. If I couldn't have her, then neither could he."

Karen prompted Cowan to recall his account of what had happened on the morning of Beth's death. He spoke about how he'd gone up there to meet her, and rather than confronting her, a rage had swelled within him as a flashback of her and Taylor had swamped his mind. He'd wanted her to suffer the same pain and humiliation he'd been through. Something had switched in his mind as he'd seen Beth nearing the top. Love had turned to anger. In a blind rage he'd cut the rope until the scream had jolted his awareness back to the present, and by then it had been too late.

At first, he'd genuinely wanted to learn to climb as a way of meeting new friends. His first lesson had gone so disastrously wrong. Consumed with shame and embarrassment he'd decided to watch rather than take part. He'd seen it as another failing in his life but hadn't figured on meeting Beth in the process.

As Karen listened to the story it became clear he'd built an unhealthy obsession and fallen in love with her. He had used every opportunity to follow her and watch from afar. A part of him had felt intrigued and turned on as he'd watched Beth and Adam have sex, but the excitement had turned to jealousy and anger as the weeks had gone by.

After presenting the rest of the evidence Karen sent him back to the cells whilst her team put together a file for the CPS.

Jade joined Karen in her office and cupped a mug of tea in her hands as she settled into the chair opposite Karen. "How do you think it will go?"

Karen rocked back and forth in her chair as nervous energy pulsed through her body. She tapped her fingers on the desk and pulled her lips into a thin line. The waiting always got to her. All they could do was find the evidence and present it to the Crown Prosecution Service. Karen hoped they'd done enough to convince the CPS that charges could be brought against Gary Cowan, if not then it was back to the drawing board.

"Your guess is as good as mine. I think we've done enough, but I've been there before with other cases and had truckloads of evidence, only to have CPS throw it out on a technicality. So it's not over till the fat lady sings!"

Jade smiled and stared down at her mug. "It always feels like a bit of an anticlimax when we're sitting around like this, don't you think?"

"Yeah, I guess. We're running on adrenaline in the final few hours of a case, so the waiting around does dampen the mood. I think it's because we're always worried that it's not going to go our way and leave us feeling like what's the point to all of this."

Jade agreed with the sentiment as they talked and reflected.

Karen's phone finally rung, the vibrations sending it rattling across her desk. "DCI Heath…" Karen's eyes narrowed as she listened intently.

Jade sat with bated breath watching Karen for any signs as to the outcome.

"Thanks for your time," Karen said as she ended the call.

"Well?" Jade asked, pulling herself to the edge of her seat.

"We've got it!" Karen jumped up from her chair and punched the air. "CPS confirmed the charges put to Cowan for the murder of Beth Hayes."

79

David and Carol Hayes clung to each other like shivering teenagers as they listened to Karen. The toll of losing their daughter had affected them in more ways than Karen could ever imagine. They looked gaunt and visibly thinner. Their eyes looked hollow and sad. *They probably haven't slept in days*, Karen thought.

The FLO had rustled up a few mugs of tea, and as Karen clutched hers between her hands, she let the news sink in that a man had been arrested and charged with the murder of their daughter. Due to their shocked expressions, Karen wasn't sure if they had heard her correctly. Their faces remained expressionless.

"I wish there was more that I could say at the moment, but we are checking and double-checking all of our evidence and making sure that we present the strongest possible case at court. My aim is to get the justice Beth deserves."

"Did Beth know the person responsible?"

"No. They had been in a climbing group together, and Beth had helped him on one or two occasions. But other than that, no, they didn't know each other socially or personally."

David stared up towards a picture of his daughter that took pride of place on their mantelpiece. "We had a faint suspicion that she may have been seeing someone recently. She was going out far more often than normal and having hushed conversations on the phone with her bedroom door closed. It wasn't him?"

"No."

"Oh, right." David hung his head and pulled his wife close to him.

Karen didn't want to reveal too much but knew it would come out in front of a jury and members of the public. Perhaps saying it now would give them more time to come to terms with it, so it didn't come as much of a shock. "She was in a relationship with someone, a married man."

David's eyes widened, and Carol gasped as she placed a hand over her chest. They searched each other's eyes looking for answers.

Karen dreaded the word tripping off her tongue and the shock it would cause. "Beth was pregnant."

Carol's eyes watered and then she began to sob. "No. No!"

"I'm afraid so. She was very early into her term and the pregnancy was a result of the relationship with the married man."

David clenched his eyes tight and breathed deeply as the grief came in waves. "Two lives…"

"I'm sorry for your loss. I really am," Karen said after answering a few questions and saying her goodbyes.

She walked back towards the car and jumped in, staring through the windscreen and swallowing hard to fight the rising tide of sadness.

"You okay?"

Karen turned towards Zac in the passenger seat.

"No, I fucking hate doing that bit," she said, casting an eye back in the direction of the house. "It's brilliant when we get a result, but then... Well, you know what I mean."

Zac placed a hand on hers and gave her a reassuring squeeze. "It is shitty. That's why we do the job. We get bad people off the streets."

"Yeah, after they've done the damage."

"Hey, listen. You got a great result, and you've done the right thing. There are a lot of officers who would have left it to the FLO to update the family. But you did it. That takes courage, compassion and respect."

"Remind me of that in the morning," Karen said as she leant over and kissed him on the lips. "I'm starving. How about we get dinner and then go back to mine? It's about time you stayed over..."

"Delrio's?"

"Perfect," Karen said as she pulled away.

SUBSCRIBE TO MY VIP GROUP

If you haven't already joined, then to say thank you for buying or downloading this book, I'd like to invite you to join my exclusive VIP group where new subscribers get some of my books for FREE. So, if you want to be notified of future releases and special offers ahead of the pack, sign up using the link below:

Subscribe to my VIP group

https://dl.bookfunnel.com/sjhhjs7ty4

CURRENT BOOK LIST

Hop over to my website for a current list of books:

http://jaynadal.com/current-books/

ABOUT THE AUTHOR

I've always had a strong passion for whodunnits, crime series and books. The more I immersed myself in it, the stronger the fascination grew.

In my spare time you'll find me in the gym, reading books from authors in my genre or enjoying walks in the forest... It's amazing what you think of when you give yourself some space.

Oh, and I'm an avid people-watcher. I just love to watch the interaction between people, their mannerisms, their way of expressing their thoughts...Weird I know, but I could spend hours engrossed in it.

I hope you enjoy the stories that I craft for you.

Printed in Dunstable, United Kingdom